THE TENACIOUS TERRIER CAPER

THE TENACIOUS TERRIER CAPER

•

(Book Eight) in The Jennifer Gray Veterinarian Mystery Series

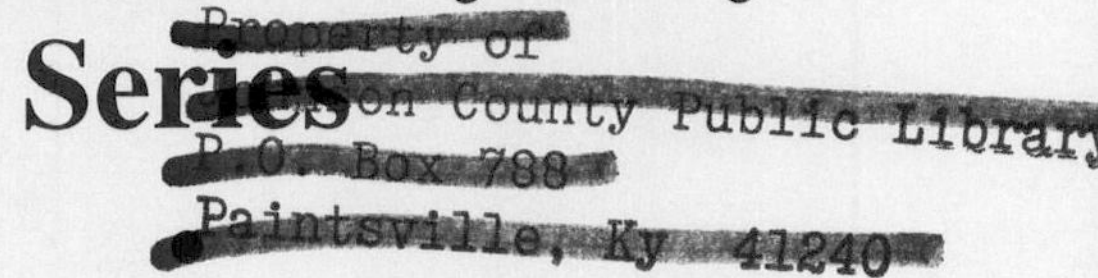

GEORGETTE LIVINGSTON

AVALON BOOKS
THOMAS BOUREGY AND COMPANY, INC.
401 LAFAYETTE STREET
NEW YORK, NEW YORK 10003

Library of Congress Catalog Card Number: 97-93731
ISBN 0-8034-9249-9

PRINTED IN THE UNITED STATES OF AMERICA
ON ACID-FREE PAPER
BY HADDON CRAFTSMEN, BLOOMSBURG, PENNSYLVANIA

For Tiger, the most tenacious Yorkie terrier of all,
and for his owners, Bonnie and Kevin,
who have their own outrageous stories to tell

Chapter One

Jennifer Gray watched the dark, angry clouds swirl overhead as Ben Copeland maneuvered the small motorboat through the murky water, and prayed the next downpour would hold off until they could rescue the shivering, frantic dog from the farmhouse roof.

The family had already been evacuated, but like the others who had been caught off guard when the lower White River levee broke, they'd had to flee for their lives, leaving behind everything they owned, including livestock and family pets.

Jennifer and Ben had taken on the job of searching for and rescuing the surviving animals, and had found it to be a formidable task at best, because so many of them had been swept away. In two days, they had found only five dogs and four cats, and it was heartbreaking.

Most of the area northwest of town was flooded, turning farmland into an endless lake, and to the east, creeks had crested, too, causing a good deal of destruction. Nor had the town been spared, as the relentless storms pushed through. Storm drains had filled beyond capacity, and many streets were under water, forcing businesses to close, which left everyone asking the same question: would their little town of Calico, Nebraska, ever be the same? Inclement weather wasn't unusual during Nebraska's fickle summers, but this series of storms seemed to be particularly brutal, and there was no letup in sight.

Shelters had been set up at the high school, the new mall east of town, and at the Calico Christian Church, where Jennifer's grandfather, Wes Gray, was pastor. And true to her loving and generous nature, Emma Morrison, who had been Wes's housekeeper for years, had taken charge at the church, preparing the food and organizing the endless work that went along with caring for so many people.

Jennifer lived with her grandfather and Emma in the little white clapboard house tucked in beside the church, and although they were only two blocks from the river, the structures had been built on higher ground, thus protecting them from any major damage.

Not so here, where the devastation seemed endless, and complete.

Ben, a tall, rugged man with a head of unruly, graying brown hair and warm hazel eyes, owned the Front Street animal clinic where Jennifer worked as his assistant. Normally, he was cheerful and upbeat, even in the face of adversity, but he wasn't smiling now. "We have company," he said, guiding the boat around a floating log before turning off the motor. "Red hair and a camera. Wonderful."

Jennifer looked over her shoulder at the

approaching motorboat, and groaned. It was Ken Hering, a reporter with *The Calico Review*, and probably about the most maddening man she'd ever met. He'd gone to college with John Wexler, Jr., son of the newspaper's founder, but instead of staying in his hometown of St. Louis, he'd come to Calico to work for his friend, who was now the managing editor. And like John, Jr., he would do anything to get a story. Jennifer supposed that kind of determination was what it took to be a good reporter, and it wasn't his fault John, Jr., had created his own brand of unimaginative, witless journalism, but did he have to be so arrogant and pushy? Their paths had crossed many times since she'd come home from veterinary school, and none of them had been pleasant experiences. Expecting this encounter to be just as bad, Jennifer braced herself. But this time, instead of the usual smirk on his face, he was frowning.

Hering slowed the boat, pulled in close, and cut the motor. "I found a horse stuck in the mud near Willow Creek," he said, using the oars to keep the boat from drifting off.

"Is there a way to get to him by car?" Jennifer asked, trying to discern the curious tone of his voice. It was almost compassionate, and not at all like him.

"Uh-huh. The other side of the creek is a little higher. A four-wheel-drive should be able to handle it, but it's going to take several able-bodied men. The horse is up to its flanks in sloppy, sandy goo."

"Then you'd better contact Max Calder at the stable," Jennifer said. "He's in charge of the rescue team for larger animals, and has made arrangements for their care."

Ben tied the boat to a bit of latticework attached to the eaves, and studied the redheaded reporter for a moment before he said, "What were you doing down at Willow Creek?"

"Shooting pictures," Hering said easily. He let go of the oars, and aimed the camera. "This is big news, and the residents have the right to see what's going on. That's why I'm out and about, braving this awful weather and so-called lake with all its hidden booby traps. You can be skimming along one minute, and the next minute you're tangled up in floating debris. Anyway, the more shots I can get, the better. Try for a smile, pretty vet lady."

Jennifer scowled instead. "Sorry, but I don't feel like smiling. And I'm sure the residents know what's going on. All they have to do is look around, or talk to the people who have taken shelter in the evacuation centers. More and more are coming in all the time, and from every location. Some of it isn't so bad, a flooded basement or a leaky roof. But then there are the real tragedies that are so sad, I can hardly stand it. This farmhouse is lost, and the Cutlers will have to rebuild from the ground up. What a way to begin a new life."

"Meaning?"

Jennifer sighed. "They've only been in Calico a few months, and just purchased the farm. The ink is hardly dry on the paper."

"They wanted a simpler way of life after living in a big city," Ben said, "and look what they got."

"Kids?"

"No," Jennifer replied. "They haven't been married long."

Hering snapped a series of photos, and grabbed the oars. “Great way to start a marriage. Are they staying at the church?”

Jennifer nodded. “That’s how we knew about their dog. Tom Cutler said they had to leave in such a hurry, they didn’t have time to look for Bosworth, so I’d say Bosworth was one lucky dog. Somehow, he managed to scramble up on the roof.”

Bosworth, a mixed breed that resembled a black Lab, heard his name and began to wiggle and yip. “That’s a good boy,” Jennifer said encouragingly. “We’ll have you down from there in a minute.”

“Let’s hope,” Ben muttered. “The house could go at any minute, and take us right along with it. The roof doesn’t look all that stable, either, so if anybody feels like saying a prayer or two, now would be the time to do it.”

“Are you taking the animals you rescue to the clinic?” Hering asked.

“That was our plan,” Jennifer returned, “but the Front Street levee is showing signs of stress, and they’re talking about evacuating that area, too. Grandfather is using the social hall at the church for the people, so we're keeping the animals in the Sunday-school room."

"That sounds cozy. Are they all running loose?"

"We have the cats and small dogs in cages or carrying cases, and the larger dogs are in portable pens."

"I assume the good pastor and Emma Morrison are taking care of the evacuees, so who's taking care of the animals while you're out here?"

Jennifer said, "Tina Allen, though there isn't much to do except make sure they have fresh water, and feed and exercise them once a day. When an animal is cooped up like that, it has the tendency to sleep a lot."

"Tina Allen. You mean the doctor's kid who sweeps the floors at the clinic?"

"Tina does much more than sweep the floors," Jennifer said indignantly. "She's our third set of hands, and someday, she's going to be a fine vet."

Ken Hering gave a little shrug. "Sorry. No offense intended. So, with the clinic off-limits, what happens if you have an emergency? You know, like an injured dog or cat?"

"We'll use the facilities at the clinic as long as we can, and pray the levee holds. The sandbagging crews are working on it today."

"Come on, boy," Ben was saying. "That's it. Take a few more steps."

The dog had inched his way down the roof, with his eyes on Ben, but he was very much aware of the swirling water. Finally, he was close enough for Ben to reach, and within moments, he was in the boat.

Jennifer quickly wrapped Bosworth in a blanket, and held him close. "That's it, sweetie," she said, looking into his dark, trusting eyes. "Just relax. We'll have you on dry ground in no time."

Hering shook his head. "You know, it's hard to believe it's only been a couple of weeks since the circus was here, and the whole town was smiling. Now, that plot of land where they were set up is under four feet of water, and everything is gloom and doom. I'll admit I don't much like circuses, but if the storm had hit while they were here, it would've been one giant disaster, what with all those animals. Just shows you, you never know from one day to the next." He looked at Jennifer slyly. "One of these days, you're going to have to tell me where you found the runaway camel, and why the Cromwell sisters ended up with the chimpanzee."

His comment finally brought a smile to Jennifer's face. "You have your secret sources for getting the news, and I have *my* secrets."

"Uh-huh, well, didn't your grandpa ever tell you that secrets were meant to be shared? The first time those crazy ladies came to town with the chimp dressed up in a pink pinafore, I couldn't believe my eyes. Couldn't get word one out of them, either. I thought about accusing them of stealing the chimp from the circus to stir things up, but I've never been good at handling pain. From what I've heard, those two can trounce a grown man on a bad day. Speaking of the Cromwell sisters, are they okay? I mean, are they high and dry?"

Surprised by the concern she could hear in his voice, Jennifer nodded. "So far, but like everybody else at that end of town, they're keeping an eye on the River Road levee."

Ken Hering looked up at the sky. "And one eye on the weather, I would imagine. Well, I'd better go find Max Calder, so he can see to the horse. And I meant what I said, Jennifer Gray. One of these days, I'm going to take you to the Hilltop Café, and by the time I've wined and dined you in fine style, you'll be willing to share all your secrets. Who knows? You might even tell me what you see in that pompous attorney who thinks he's going to be mayor."

Jennifer flung out, "Pompous? Boy, is *that* like the pot calling the kettle black, or what?"

Amusement flickered in his eyes. "Is that your way of calling me pompous?"

"Among other things. And you're wrong. Willy Ashton doesn't just *think* he's going to be mayor, he's *going* to be the mayor. He's running a good, clean campaign, has a sound platform, and doesn't have to resort to using underhanded tactics like Elmer Dodd. And one day very soon, Elmer is going to realize that just because he has a lot of money and owns the dairy, he can't buy votes. Nor will you find Willy campaigning during this horrible crisis. He's out sandbagging and doing everything he can to help."

"As opposed to?"

"As opposed to Elmer Dodd and his condescending campaign manager, who just happens to be his nephew. They are going around to the shelters, shaking hands, making speeches, and blowing smoke."

Hering chuckled and made a mark in the air with his finger. "Elmer and Collin Dodd, blowing smoke. May I quote you?"

"Do what you want. You will anyway."

Jennifer could have come back at him with a dozen different reasons why she was so fond of her longtime friend Willy Ashton, and why he was going to win the mayoral race, but what would be the point? *The Calico Review* and its employees were backing Elmer Dodd all the way, and now wasn't the time for a political debate.

"That's right," Hering said, starting the motor. "I will anyway. *Ciao.*"

Ben watched the reporter maneuver the

motorboat through the water, and frowned. "If I didn't know better, I'd say he just asked you for a date."

Jennifer rolled her eyes. "That'll be the day. He's been my nemesis for the last year, Ben, and that isn't going to change. Let's go back to town and reunite Bosworth with his family, and give Tina a break. Between all the cats yowling and the dogs barking, she's probably going crazy."

Ben smiled for the first time in hours. "Knowing Tina, she's probably read them all a bedtime story and has them snoozing peacefully. But it's time *we* had a break, young lady, and right about now, a cup of Emma's coffee sounds pretty good. And I want to call Irene. She said she was going out sandbagging today, and I'll tell you, that has me a little concerned. I tried to remind her she's sixty, not thirty, and I thought I was going to be the recipient of flying pots and pans."

Jennifer grinned. "I wouldn't worry, Ben. Irene is a strong lady, in mind and spirit. Your house has been spared, so I can understand why she wants to help the less fortunate. If Emma wasn't working at the church, she'd be out sandbagging, too, or maybe directing traffic through the miniature lake that's developed at the intersection of Jefferson and Main."

"Jefferson and Main, huh? That's pretty close to the courthouse and the town square."

"I know. If it keeps up, the whole town is going to come to a standstill. . . ." Jennifer broke off, unable to go on. Overhead the sky had darkened, and she felt the first drops of rain.

"Lordy, just look at you!" Emma exclaimed, handing Jennifer and Ben large, fluffy towels. "I told your granddaddy you weren't going to make it back before the next downpour. Well, at least you found the Cutlers' dog. Now all we have to do is find the Cutlers. Alice had a bit of an upset stomach, and Tom took her for a walk. That was two hours ago."

"Maybe they're directing traffic at the intersection of Jefferson and Main," Ben said, wiping his face with the towel. When he saw

Emma's puzzled expression, he grinned. "Just a little humor there, Emma. Where's Tina?"

"She had to leave. Her daddy called, and said the hospital parking lot is flooded. That's pretty close to their house, and he thought Tina should be home with her mama. She felt bad about leaving, but the animals have been little angels, so I encouraged her to go."

A frown creased Ben's brow. "The hospital isn't too far from my house, either. Have you heard from Irene?"

Emma said, "No, we surely haven't. Best you go home, too, Ben Copeland, and save all the animal rescues for another day."

Ben gave Jennifer a hug. "God willing, I'll see you in the morning, Jennifer."

Jennifer returned his hug. "Be careful?"

Ben nodded, and hurried out.

Emma sighed. "If it isn't one thing, it's another. Like that couple who came in while you were gone. Perkins. Millie and Fred Perkins, and they're just the nicest people. They live in Scottsbluff and were on their way to Omaha, taking the scenic tour, when they got caught in a flash flood just outside Calico. Now, their car is stuck in the mud, so here they are, marooned like everybody else. They have a cute little doggie, too. A Yorkshire terrier named Tootsie Marie. Supposedly they named her after some lady wrestler because Tootsie Marie thinks she's every bit as big and tough as a one-hundred-pound German shepherd, even if she does have to wear a bow on her head to keep all that long hair out of her eyes."

Jennifer looked around the room. "So where is the dog?"

"With the Perkinses. They keep her right in the carrying case, and won't let it out of their sight."

"Well, if there are any complaints from the other evacuees during the night, they might end up sleeping in here."

"Don't think they'd mind at all." Emma blew at a strand of brown, wiry hair that had fallen over her forehead, and smoothed down her flowered apron. "The sheriff stopped by earlier. He said the highway is closed in both directions, so even if the tow truck driver can get to the Perkinses' car, they aren't going anywhere. Oh, and the sheriff brought along some sad news. Nettie Balkin's house is flooded out. I told the sheriff she's welcome to stay here, but you know Nettie. She's been the sheriff's right hand so long, she couldn't walk away from the job if she wanted to. She's staying at the sheriff's office so she can handle the phones and dispatch. Says she'll worry about the house later."

Jennifer's heart twisted at the thought of Nettie's lovely house under water. "The flood has touched just about everybody, Emma, in one way or another. Other than the Perkinses, do we have any new evacuees?"

"A few. Linda and Ed Peterson arrived a couple of hours ago. They never did get around to putting a new roof on the farmhouse, and they say it's leaking pretty bad."

"And the boys?"

Emma shook her head. "They're spending the summer with their grandma in Texas. About all we can do is pray they have a house to come back to. Deputy Pressman's wife, Kathy, is here with their new little baby, and Jack Boodie arrived about a half hour ago."

"Boodie's Roadhouse is flooded?"

"Not yet, but water has reached the entrance. Oh, and we have Zeke and Nora Muller, Charlie Waters and his wife, Margie, Norman Fuller, and old Doc Chambers. Norman Fuller, like the Cutlers, has been flooded out, but then I guess we should've expected it, since he lives next door to Nettie. Zeke and Nora are here as a precaution. Their pond is spreading out in all directions, and is inching pretty close to the house. The Pressmans can't get down the road to their house, and it's the same with Charlie and Margie. Old Doc Chambers? He claims his roof is going to start leaking any minute, but if you want my opinion, I think he just wants to be a part of it all, or maybe he needs some reassuring. The sheriff said the high school and mall are running about the same as far as attendance, but if this keeps up . . . Well, we can't change things, so we'd better make the best of it."

Jennifer listened to the rain pound down

on the roof, and shivered. "So, how is everybody handling it?"

"About like you'd expect. Doesn't help to have old Doc Chambers stirring everybody up with his tales of woe. And he isn't talking about the weather. He's talking about his practice getting dumped into the garbage after they built the hospital. I'd love to remind him he's eighty going on one hundred and ten, and couldn't find the right end of a stethoscope if he tried, but I figure I'd better stay out of it."

"You didn't mention Norman Fuller's wife."

"Supposedly, she's in South Dakota, visiting a sister. You talk to Nettie, though, and she'll tell you a different story. But then, she's been living next door to him for five or six years, and has her own opinions."

Jennifer laughed. "I know. He looks like Norman Bates; Nettie hasn't seen the wife in years, and figures he has her stashed in the basement, living on bread and water."

Emma's eyes twinkled. "Well, Nettie is right. He looks just like Norman Bates. When he wasn't dressed up to look like his dead mama, that is. I still have nightmares about that *Psycho* movie, and for a long time, I wouldn't take a shower."

"That's the way I feel about *The Shining.* Every time I see a hatchet, I think of Jack Nicholson. Is Grandfather in the social hall?"

"He is. When I left, he was refereeing a heated discussion about the mayoral race. And believe me, it was a room divided. Well, like I've always said, stick a bunch of people in the middle of a crisis, and you'll find out their true colors."

"Then we'd better go rescue him, Emma."

"You go on ahead. I've got three pans of lasagna in the church ovens, and it's time to toss the salad. Just don't tell anybody what I'm doing. Otherwise, I'll have all the ladies in the kitchen trying to help, and driving me crazy. I don't mind help with the cleanup, you understand, but when you get a bunch of clucking, opinionated females together, all trying to put in their two cents about what's supposed to go in the stew pot, well, that's when I have to put my foot down. Your granddaddy is a patient man, and I'd like to think I'm a patient lady, but I'll tell you right now, things are getting a bit testy." When thunder cracked overhead, Emma shuddered. "Lordy, when is this going to end!"

Jennifer was about to give Emma an encouraging hug, when Wes walked in, trying to contain his laughter. He was a tall, handsome man, with a head of white, wavy hair, and blue eyes, and as always, just the sight of him made Jennifer feel better.

"I talked to Ben on his way out, so I knew you were here," Wes said, kissing Jennifer's cheek. "Thought I'd better warn you before you head for the social hall. Jack Boodie and Norman Fuller are ready to duke it out, and Margie Waters is all set to take on Linda Peterson."

Emma sniffed. "And you think that's funny?"

"It's like a corny joke, Emma. You have to hear it in person to appreciate it."

Emma harrumphed. "So, did the Cutlers come back?"

"Nope, not yet. Think I should go look for them?"

Emma snorted. “In this weather? No way. About as far as you’re going to go is to the kitchen when it’s time to carry in the lasagna pans. That’s it!”

Wes watched Emma march out of the room, and his eyes softened as he spoke to Jennifer. “She’s done a lot more than a body should have to do, sweetheart, and yet she won’t let anybody help her with the cooking.”

“And she won’t either, because cooking is like therapy for her. It probably even adds a bit of normalcy to things, and it definitely gets her away from the dissenters.”

Wes looked down at Bosworth, and smiled. “I see we have a new addition. The Cutlers’ dog?”

“Yes. He was stranded on the roof, Grandfather, and the house . . .” Jennifer took a deep breath. “Water is right up to the eaves.”

Wes shook his head sadly. “We’ve been listening to the radio for updates, and we heard about all that farmland going under. Grief takes many forms. Maybe that’s why the Cutlers wanted to be alone. For sure, that's why I haven't intervened in the heated debates going on in the social hall. Like Emma feels the need to cook, arguing is a way for those folks to let off steam. I figure when they get it out of their systems, they'll be ready for a few prayers. Might even get them to shake hands and make up."

"Are you going to spend the night in the social hall to keep an eye on things?" Jennifer asked.

"Won't have to. Deputy Pressman will be here before long, and I think he'll be able to handle our boarders just fine. And if he can't, I'll only be a couple of hundred yards away. What about you? Do you plan on spending the night with the animals?"

"I have to, Grandfather, in the event we have any unforeseen accidents or emergencies. I'll set up a cot and use a sleeping bag, so it won't be so bad."

"Well, if you need me, be sure and let me know." Wes sniffed the air. "I smell lasagna. Shall we set out the paper plates?"

"I thought Emma wanted to use the church dishes so everybody would feel more at home."

Wes gave her a wink. "Well, I think we'd be a lot safer using paper plates, in the event they decide to throw things."

"Oh, Grandfather, are things *that* bad?"

"No, but it wouldn't take much. Trust me."

Jennifer shook her head, and followed Wes down the hall.

Chapter Two

The social hall, a large airy room used primarily for potluck suppers and wedding receptions, was lined with cots, bedding, and sleeping bags on one side, and folding tables and chairs on the other. The heavy, mustard-colored drapes had been pulled over the windows to block out the storm, and the air was filled with the aroma of damp clothing, wood smoke from the potbellied stove in the corner, and Emma's lasagna. It was also a room that should have been filled with the camaraderie of sharing grief and misfortune. Instead, it was immersed in hostility and chaos as tempers flared, and patience ran thin. Only Millie and Fred Perkins were smiling, trying to make the best of their impossible situation, even though, like most of the other evacuees, they were dressed in mismatched, ill-fitting, donated clothing.

The Perkinses were a cute, plumpish couple in their early sixties, and Jennifer liked them immediately. And Tootsie Marie liked Jennifer. Because Fred Perkins seemed hesitant to take the little dog out of the carrying case, Jennifer had gotten acquainted with her through the bars on the door by stroking her gray-brown silky coat, and scratching her under her pert little chin.

At the moment, Jennifer was sitting with the Perkinses at one of the corner tables, wondering which was worse—the unrelenting storm that had knocked out power twice during supper, or the peevish moods that seemed to be going from bad to worse.

Tootsie gave a frustrated yip, and Millie Perkins looked at the little dog with a sigh. "I keep telling Fred to take Tootsie Marie to that room where you're keeping the animals so she can get some exercise, but he won't hear of it. Poor little thing just doesn't know what to make of all this upheaval. The only time we ever put her in the carrying case is when she has to be in the car, and yet she hasn't seen the inside of the car for hours."

"Tootsie Marie will be just fine, Mama," Fred said firmly. "I've been taking her out under the church overhang every couple of hours, and she doesn't look all that upset to me." He nodded at Wes, who was now refereeing an after-supper debate between Charlie Waters and Doc Chambers. "That grandpa of yours has the patience of ten men, Jennifer. I know this is a difficult time, and everybody is a bit touchy, but from what I've observed, these people seem more interested in the mayoral race than the storm. Mind you, it isn't my place to speak up, but if the whole town gets swept away by the flood, it won't matter who's elected mayor."

Millie frowned. "That's right, it isn't your place, Papa. How would you feel if some stranger popped up on our doorstep in Scottsbluff, and told you what he thought was wrong with our town, or how we should run it? Just be thankful that nice tow truck driver was willing to bring us to the church. And you would do well to spend your time praying that he can get our vehicle out of the mud, and the roads open up, so we can be on our way. And be thankful, too, we were able to call James and let him know why we've been delayed." She sighed. "James is our son in Omaha, Jennifer. Don't know if Emma or your grandpa told you, but we were on the way for a visit when we were caught in that flash flood. Now *that* was an experience I don't want to go through again. Why, I . . ."

Millie's words trailed off as Norman Fuller's voice rose above the others. "I don't care what you say, Peterson. How long have you been livin' in Calico? Six months? A year? That sure don't entitle you to tell *me* what this town needs. I say we dam up Willow Creek, and this sort of thing won't happen again. Elmer Dodd agrees, and that's one of the reasons why I'm voting for him."

Ed Peterson returned, "I've been here long enough to know a crook when I see one, and they don't make them any bigger than Elmer Dodd. Have you thought about what damming up the creek will do to the farmers at that end of town? No, of course you haven't. You're not a farmer, and neither is Dodd."

"Well, you ain't a farmer, either," Norman shot back. "Just because you bought the old McGovern farm, don't make you a farmer. The last I heard, those two teenage sons of yours are using the cornfield for a football, baseball, and soccer field, depending on the season, and you're using the barn and outbuildings for storage. And as far as those farms near Willow Creek are concerned, most of them are gone anyway, or they will be by the time the storm pushes on. And I'll tell you somethin' else. It don't take bein' a farmer to lose everything. Me and my wife just lost our house. So what have you got? A leaky roof. Big deal."

Ed Peterson countered with, "Our farm is also close to Fox Creek, and *it* could crest at any time."

Norman frowned. "I've lived in Calico going on six years now, and I've seen many a storm. And not once has Fox Creek flooded its banks."

When Wes stepped over to the sparring

twosome, Millie shook her head. "Your grandpa is going to have to work a miracle to keep those two apart, Jennifer. Same with Mr. Fuller and Mr. Boodie. I've come to the conclusion Mr. Fuller just plain likes to argue, no matter what. Some people are like that." Her eyes narrowed in thought. "You know, Mr. Fuller looks so familiar. I just know I've seen him somewhere before. I talked to Emma about it, and her reaction was a bit puzzling, to say the least. It was the first time I've seen her smile all day."

Jennifer was wondering if she should tell Millie that Norman Fuller looked like Norman Bates in *Psycho,* when Fred cleared his throat and said, "I don't think anybody in Calico has all that much to smile about, Mama. Especially Norman Fuller and the Cutlers. They've lost everything. They're just handling it in a different way, that's all. Norman Fuller is angry, and the Cutlers are sad, but to my way of thinking, it means the same thing. I surely hope Mrs. Cutler is feeling better."

Millie retorted, "Well, I think she'd feel a whole lot better if she got into some of that dry clothing the church people provided. She'd feel better, too, if she ate some of Emma's lasagna, and cuddled over there by the nice warm stove instead of hibernating in that cold room with the animals. Don't think Mr. Cutler should've taken her out for that walk, either, no matter how poorly she was feeling. She was wet clean through when they came back, shaking like a leaf, and she's probably going to catch her death."

Fred scowled. "Now who's putting their nose in where it doesn't belong?"

"Well, it's true. I also think we should be doing more to help out. There must be *something* we can do to get everybody's mind off all their trials and tribulations. The pastor tried organizing some games, and that didn't work. I'd suggest we have a sing-along, but with the ladies in the kitchen trying to help Emma clean up, we'd only have the crotchety men, and not one of them looks like the sing-along type to me." She patted Jennifer's hand. "I'd be in the kitchen helping out, too, but Emma wouldn't hear of it."

Jennifer smiled at the rosy-cheeked little

woman. "Emma has more than enough help, Millie. If she didn't, she'd let you know."

"Well, I'm not so sure about that. Emma strikes me as the kind of lady—" A screech outside the door stopped her in midsentence. She gave a little gasp, then cried, "My word, what was that!"

Jennifer caught her grandfather's eye, and he was grinning from ear to ear. It was Peaches, the chimp, which meant the Cromwell sisters couldn't be far behind.

Moments later, they burst through the door, struggling with oversized satchels, the chimp, and a large black umbrella. Visualizing the incredible scene through Millie and Fred's eyes brought a smile to Jennifer's face. Frances and Fanny Cromwell were tall, large-boned women with wild gray hair, leathery skin, and startling blue eyes. Both wore granny glasses, and their outfits were always the same, no matter what the weather: long black dresses trimmed in cream-colored lace, and black, calf-high boots. Wondering what Millie and Fred would say if they knew the ladies were known as "the crazy Cromwell sisters," made moonshine in a bathtub, and were probably carrying a supply of it in their satchels, Jennifer announced, "I think our dilemma has been solved, Millie. If anybody can make the evacuees forget about their problems, it's those three."

Before Jennifer, or Wes, could make a move in their direction, the sisters spied Jennifer, and marched over to the table. "Here's pretty Jennifer Gray!" Fanny exclaimed. "Oh, and here comes the pastor. Stop that, Peaches. You promised you'd be good!"

Peaches, dressed in blue coveralls, was struggling to get out of Fanny's arms. Jennifer took Peaches from Fanny, and hugged her close. Long arms wrapped around Jennifer's neck. Next came the low chortling sounds in the chimp's throat, while she made a series of comical faces, showing lots of teeth. She was showing off for her audience, and loving every minute of it.

"You little dickens," Jennifer said, giving Peaches a hug.

"Well, this is a pleasant surprise," Wes said, reaching out to pat the chimp on the head. "But I sure hope it doesn't mean you've been flooded out."

Frances shoved her granny glasses up on her nose, and gave a healthy grunt. "So far, that River Road levee is holding, but we've got us a leak in the kitchen. It was last Christmas season when Fanny shot a hole in the kitchen ceiling. Well, you know all about that, Pastor Wes. You and your pretty young granddaughter were right there with us when it happened. Well, seeing as how we rent that cottage, we decided not to tell the landlord."

Fanny spoke up. "Harold Swartzel. He's that crabby old man who owns that pig farm out on Hollow Road."

"That's Swallow Road, Sister, and his first name is Harvey, not Harold. Harold owns the garage out by the new shopping center. You know, the man who sold us that ragtag truck. Anyway, when Fanny blew a hole in the kitchen ceiling, we decided to fix it ourselves. Now it's leaking, and if this storm keeps up, we're afraid the whole ceiling is going to come down. You have to understand, we're not all that concerned for ourselves. Wouldn't be the first time we had a bit of falling plaster, but Peaches plays in the kitchen all the time, and we surely don't want anything to happen to her."

"Our old dirt road is gettin' pretty bad, too," Fanny said. "We was afraid of gettin' stuck in the mud if we waited any longer. 'Course, the high school and shoppin' center was closer to our little cottage, but we wanted to be here with all our good friends." She looked around the room, and scowled. "Hmm. Don't see many friendly faces. Is that old Doc Chambers? Hmm. Thought he died years ago." She looked down at Millie and Fred. "Howdy. Haven't seen you two before."

Jennifer made introductions, noted the look of disbelief on the Perkinses' faces, like they didn't quite believe what they were seeing, and smiled. "And this is Peaches. She's a wonderful chimpanzee, who is simply a delight."

Millie coughed. "Ah, well, I can't help but wonder how . . . Well, isn't a chimpanzee a rather strange pet to have in the middle of Nebraska's farm belt?"

Frances looked down her nose at Millie. "Calico isn't in the middle of Nebraska's farm belt. It's too far north. We might do farming, but we've got lots of waterways and trees and hills and even a big game refuge not more than thirty miles to the north."

Millie nodded. "Ah, so that's where you got the chimp."

Fanny's heavy brows drew together in a scowl. "They don't have chimpanzees on the game refuge. They've got bison, elk, deer, Texas Longhorn cattle, skunks, raccoons, beavers, coyotes, and bobcats."

Millie sniffed. "Well, we know all about game refuges. We live in Scottsbluff, and have the Wildcat Hills Game Refuge. We also have Scotts Bluff, which is a prominent landmark on the Oregon Trail, and we have that wonderful Chimney Rock National Park."

"So, did you have Buffalo Bill Cody a-stayin' in one of your houses?" Fanny returned indignantly. "He stayed right there in one of those houses near White River Bridge while his house was bein' built in North Platte, and everybody knows he had a secret meetin' with Chief Crazy Horse. We got us a museum, too, full of art-tee-facts, and a history that goes back a lot further than the Oregon Trail."

Wes cleared his throat. "The ladies got Peaches from a friend, Millie, and that little cutie will be bringing a lot of sunshine into their lives, as well as ours.

"Have you two eaten?" he asked the sisters.

Fanny patted her satchel. "Have everything we need right here."

Frances nodded. "We didn't come to take up space and eat your food, Pastor Wes. We came because our roof is leaking and we want to help out. I see some pretty glum faces around this room. Don't know that man with the long face and strange eyes, but I recognize most of the others, and I think we should do something to brighten their spirits. This is a time when neighbors are supposed to be pulling together."

"His name is Norman Fuller," Wes said. "His house was flooded, along with all the houses on his street. That includes Nettie

Balkin's old house that has withstood every storm since it was built."

"My oh my, Sister, you hear that? Nettie Balkin's house was flooded. What a shame. So where is she?"

"At the sheriff's office," Jennifer said.

Fanny bobbed her head. "I heard. The storm ain't playin' no favorites, that's for sure. Well, I guess the sheriff needs Nettie's help along about now, and she can always sleep in one of the jail cells. Maybe we can help her out later. We could even put her up in our spare room, if she has a mind to. Now, I think I'll start by helpin' that poor man with the long face." She frowned. "Don't see any ladies, but for that pretty little gal over in the corner with the baby."

Wes said, "That's Kathy Pressman, Deputy Pressman's wife. The rest of the ladies are in the church kitchen, helping Emma with the dishes. By the way, if you decide you're hungry later on, I'm sure Emma has some of her fine lasagna left over."

Fanny sniffed the air, and her nose twitched. "I can smell it. Too bad I wasn't here when she was makin' it. Nobody makes lasagna better than me. Got me some secret ingredients." She took the chimp's hand. "Come along, Peaches. Let's see if we can cheer up that gloomy man."

Fred watched Peaches amble across the floor beside Fanny, and shook his head. "The last time I saw a chimpanzee was in a circus. Think it was Omaha, or maybe it was Lincoln. That was a long time ago. Too long. There is something about a circus that brings out the kid in everybody. Think I'll take Tootsie Marie out front for a breath of fresh air."

Fred took the Yorkie out of the carrying case, and Frances smiled. "Well, now, that's a mighty fine-looking dog you have there. You say her name is Tootsie Marie? Had a friend once named Marie. 'Peaches Marie.' That sounds nice. Maybe we should change that rascal's name. We put bows in Peaches's hair, too, when she's wearing a pinafore. A different color bow for each dress."

"I'll take Tootsie Marie out if you'd like," Jennifer offered. "I could use some fresh air myself."

Fred snapped the leash on Tootsie Marie's collar, and nodded. "I appreciate the offer. Just don't let her get in the mud. She gets mud in her coat and it takes forever and a day to comb it out."

Outside, finally, with the little dog standing obediently beside her, Jennifer stayed under the protection of the overhang, and breathed in deeply of the damp evening air. The wind had let up a little, as well as the rain, and she could even see a break in the clouds overhead.

Jennifer closed her eyes and prayed for a lot of things, but mostly for a quick end to the cruel storm that had caused so much destruction. She was so intent, she wasn't aware of the sheriff's approaching footsteps, until he said, "Let's see if I remember. Her name is Tootsie Marie, and she belongs to the couple from Scottsbluff."

Sheriff Jim Cody was a large man with thinning gray hair, and had been the sheriff as long as Jennifer could remember. He was also a good friend. Jennifer turned and smiled. "Hi, Sheriff Cody. You're right on all counts. You look exhausted."

He took off his olive-green hat, and ran a weary hand through his hair. "I am. I only have eight deputies, so I've had to employ the use of the auxiliary fire department. Between sandbagging, traffic jams, fender benders, and power outages, I could use a few more dozen helping hands. And if that isn't enough, we've had some looting."

"Looting? Oh, no!"

"Yeah, well, you can't be any more surprised than I am. Good Lord, Jennifer, don't these poor people have enough to deal with? Guess I'd better tell you. That reporter, Ken Hering, isn't far behind me. Since he found out about the looting, he's been following me all over. Anything for a story. And you'll be seeing Elmer and Collin Dodd pretty soon, too. Saw them driving down Main Street, and they were headed this way. From what I understand, they've spent most of the day shaking hands, promising the moon to our distraught citizens, and making a nuisance of themselves in general." He sighed. "About the looting. It was the jewelry store. The culprit about cleaned the place out of diamond rings and gold jewelry. We evacuated that area of town earlier today, but in the confusion, the Kirchers didn't lock up. Ron thought Evie had locked up, and Evie thought Ron had locked up, and in the process, the door was left open. Well, at least it was wide open when Ron went back later for some important papers. No signs of forced entry."

"That's really terrible, Sheriff. Who would do something like that at a time like this?"

The sheriff gave her a wan smile. "I think you're the one who told me not too long ago that *everything* seems to happen in Calico. We'll dust for fingerprints, but I don't expect much out of that. The jewelry store is open to the public, and probably half the town has been in there shopping at one time or another, and when you take into consideration all the tourists who come through during the summer months, well, I don't expect to find the culprit that way. To tell you the truth, I don't expect to find him at all." Another sigh. "Was that the Cromwell sisters' truck I saw out in the parking lot?"

Jennifer grinned. "It was. They have a leaky kitchen roof."

"And Peaches?"

"They brought her along. Hopefully, they'll be able to put a smile on some pretty gloomy faces."

"Uh-huh, well, did they bring along their satchels?"

Jennifer chuckled. "They did."

"Then I'd say it's guaranteed. Oh-oh. What did I tell you? Here he comes. Stall him for a few minutes until I can talk to your grandfather?"

Jennifer nodded. "Send Grandfather out when it's all clear."

Ken Hering, wearing a rain slicker and boots, was making his way up the path beside the church, oblivious to the puddles. "Well, this is a nice surprise," he said, giving Jennifer a broad smile. "I get to see your pretty face twice in one day. I saw the sheriff before he ducked inside, so I know he told you he thinks I'm following him around to get a scoop on the robbery, but I planned to stop by the church anyway. I want some photos to finish out the day. I've already been to the mall, and now it's your turn. One thing. Elmer and Collin Dodd are out front, looking for a place to park. I told them I thought it was pretty gutsy to come here when they know it's the enemy camp. They said being gutsy is how elections are won."

"And I suppose you're going to be right there with your camera, to catch the fall-out?"

"It's been a long day, Jennifer. Humor me?"

Jennifer sighed. "Did you get in touch with Max Calder?"

"I did, and they got the horse out of the mud. Then I spent the afternoon sandbagging. Had a choice. The Front Street levee, or the River Road levee. Picked the Front Street levee, because if it goes, so does your clinic."

Jennifer felt an unexpected tightness in her throat. "Have you eaten?"

"Two candy bars, a soda, and a bag of peanuts."

"Well, I think we can do better than that, if you don't mind leftover lasagna."

His smile lit up his face. "You have no idea how good that sounds. Is that one of the dogs you rescued?"

Tootsie Marie looked up at Ken and cocked her head. "No, she belongs to a couple from Scottsbluff who got caught in a flash flood. I'm sure they would be more than happy to tell you all about their harrowing experience."

"Who else is inside?"

Jennifer told him, then added, "The Cromwell sisters are here, too, Ken, and I know they'd be delighted to pose for pictures."

Ken eyed her intently. "Are you saying that out of the side of your mouth? Or are you serious?"

"Out of the side of my mouth, I guess. But to tell you the truth, I don't know how they'll react to you, or the camera. You just never know with them."

"Uh-huh, and they can do great bodily harm." He lowered his eyes, and kicked at an imaginary rock. "And, is Willy Ashton here?"

"No. He's helping out at the high school tonight. Why?"

"Just wondered. Well, nuts. You want honest?"

"That would be nice."

"Okay, honest. I'd kinda like to be able to talk to you without Willy glaring me down."

"Sounds like he intimidates you."

"It isn't that, exactly, but I've never believed in stepping on another guy's romantic toes, if you know what I mean."

Jennifer grinned. "I've never thought of my toes as being romantic."

"And I think I'd better stop while I'm ahead. Shall we go in?"

"You want honest?" Jennifer asked.

He gave her a lopsided grin. "That would be nice."

"I'm supposed to keep you out here until the sheriff talks to my grandfather. When Grandfather comes out, we can go in."

"Uh-huh, well, I never thought of myself as having big ears, either. Just shows you. Sometimes, we don't know ourselves at all. Okay, you tell me about your day, I'll tell you about mine, and by that time, we should get the all clear."

Elmer and Collin Dodd had just rounded the corner of the church, and Jennifer shook her head. "On second thought, we'd better go in now. Grandfather should have a little forewarning that we're about to be invaded."

"If you want to go on in, I'll stall them for a few minutes," Ken said, looking over his shoulder. "See, I've always believed even the enemy should have some time to prepare for battle."

Jennifer gave him a grateful nod, and hurried inside.

Chapter Three

"Lordy, if that isn't the ticket," Emma muttered. "A robbery at a time like this? Why, who would do such a terrible thing? And the poor Kirchers. They've put every cent they have into that jewelry store, and Evie Kircher told me just the other day they've been trying to get a loan. She didn't go into details, you understand, but I got the impression they were a cat's whisker away from losing everything."

Emma had managed to shoo the women into the social hall a few minutes earlier, so Jennifer and Emma were alone in the church kitchen. At the moment, Emma was folding damp towels, with a look of pure frustration on her face. "Those ladies used up twelve towels, and they still didn't get everything dry. And they about drove me crazy, too. Nora Muller wanted to rearrange the cupboards, and all Margie Waters could do was complain about the inconvenience of being 'homeless.' I tried to tell her, her house isn't flooded, just the road getting to it, but she wouldn't listen. Then Margie and Linda Peterson started arguing politics, and I finally kicked them all out." Emma sighed. "I know, it probably isn't any better in the social hall. It makes a body wonder where it's going to end, that's for sure. Did the sheriff say if he's had supper? I have quite a bit of lasagna left over, and some salad."

"He didn't say, Emma, but Ken Hering hasn't eaten, so I'd like to fix him a plate."

"Ken Hering? What's *he* doing here?"

"The sheriff says Ken has been following him around all day, trying to get information about the robbery, but Ken says he's here to take some pictures for the paper, so your guess is as good as mine."

Emma announced with a scowl, "Well, he isn't taking a picture of me!"

Jennifer took the pan of lasagna out of the oversized refrigerator, put a generous portion on a plate, and had it in the microwave before she said, "There's more, Emma. Elmer and Collin Dodd are here, too."

Emma harrumphed. "Well, I guess that shouldn't be a surprise. I figured they'd get around to coming here sooner or later. Don't tell me; let me guess. Mutt and Jeff are wearing those ridiculous cream-colored suits, and don't have a speck of mud on 'em."

Jennifer smiled at Emma's comical description. Elmer was as short and fat as Collin was tall and thin, but they looked a lot alike, especially around the eyes and nose, and both men wore their black hair slicked back, and had a penchant for white or cream-colored suits, straw hats, and an overabundance of gold jewelry, usually worn in the form of watches, tie tacks, stickpins, and watch fobs. "You're partially right. They're wearing their infamous linen suits, but they look like they've found every mud hollow in town. Grandfather made them take off their shoes, and both men had holes in their socks."

Emma tittered. "Well, I guess it takes something like this to make all men equal. Guess we'd better go help your granddaddy referee. I can see one colossal debate coming up."

Jennifer gave Emma a sly grin. "Everything is under control, Emma. The Cromwell sisters are here with Peaches, and from what I've seen, Elmer Dodd is scared to death of them."

Emma rolled her eyes. "That's all we need. The nutty Cromwell sisters, stirring things up. Did they get flooded out?"

"Remember that time Fanny shot a hole in the kitchen ceiling? Well, they were afraid to tell the landlord, and fixed it themselves. Now, it's leaking. Actually, I think they'll be a big help, Emma. Just their presence has a stabilizing influence, and they aren't afraid of hard work."

Emma harrumphed. "Well, if Elmer Dodd is scared to death of them, guess I can put up with their shenanigans. Poor Millie and Fred Perkins must think our town is full of lunatics and oddballs. Hmm. Well, it'll be a treat seeing little Peaches again. Is she wearing a pinafore?"

"No, she's wearing blue coveralls."

"Hmm. Well, remind me to give the sisters that box of material I've got stored in the hall closet. It's mostly odds and ends, but there should be enough there to make Peaches a couple of nice little dresses."

Jennifer gave Emma a hug. "Our town is also full of wonderful people, and you're at the top of the list, Emma."

Emma flushed rosy pink. "Ah-ha, well, I guess I'd better live up to that compliment, and put a smile on my face. Do you think that reporter would like a roll to go along with his supper?"

It took Jennifer only a moment to discern that something significant must have happened when she walked into the social hall with Emma a few minutes later. With the exception of the Cromwell sisters, who were standing in the middle of the room like a couple of schoolmarms, everybody was seated, including Elmer and Collin Dodd. No one was talking, or arguing, and the silence was almost tangible. Wes was sitting with the Perkinses with Peaches in his lap, but it wasn't until he winked at her and she caught his amused expression, that she realized what had happened. The Cromwell sisters had taken charge.

Frances looked at Jennifer and Emma, and clapped her hands. "Well, now that Jennifer Gray and Emma Morrison are here, we can get on with the festivities."

Fanny scowled. "We ain't havin' a party, Sister. We're havin' a political debate." She scowled at Elmer and Collin Dodd. "Wouldn't be havin' that if *those* two hadn't showed up, tryin' to drum up votes."

An outburst followed, with everybody talking at once, and Fanny whistled through her teeth. When silence fell over the crowd again, she announced, "And we ain't gonna have none of that! That kind of silly behavior is why we had to set up rules and regulations in the first place. Now, as soon as Jennifer and Emma take a seat, everybody will get their turn to talk. Elmer Dodd came here tonight to make a speech, and we're gonna let him make it. And after he answers all your questions, he'll be on his way. Ain't that right, Mr. Dodd?"

Elmer grimaced, but nodded.

"Good! And then we can get on with cheering up these fine folks so they won't have to think about that nasty old storm and what's a-happenin' to our fine town."

Jennifer placed the tray of food on the table in front of Ken Hering, sat down beside him, and gave him a helpless shrug. "Have at it, if you still have an appetite," she whispered.

Ken made a motion with his hand, like he was zippering his mouth shut, but she could see the merriment dancing in his eyes. Like her grandfather, he obviously found the situation more than amusing.

Frances spoke up. "Mr. Dodd, you can have the floor for exactly three minutes. Sister, get out your pocket watch."

Elmer Dodd stood up, cleared his throat, and said, "No matter what some of you think, I came here tonight to see how everybody is doing, and if I can be of any help.

This is a sad time for our little town, and we must all work together."

Mutterings could be heard throughout the crowd, and Fanny stomped a booted foot. "You'll all get your turn. Go on, Mr. Dodd."

"Ahem, well, like I said, we must all work together. I can understand why tempers are short, but nothing can be accomplished by bickering. When I become mayor, I plan to see that nothing like this ever happens again. When I become mayor, our little town will prosper under my guidance and experience. When I become mayor, each and every one of you will know what progress really means. When I become mayor . . ."

"Your time is up," Fanny announced. "Zeke Muller, you had your hand raised?"

Zeke Muller stood up. "Get off it, Dodd. You should be saying, *'if'* you become mayor, not 'when' you become mayor. And if you really care so much about our good citizens and the town, why weren't you out there today sandbagging, and working beside the people instead of trying to take advantage of them? And why haven't you donated dairy products to the shelters? The market and

Mercantile have been more than generous, so what's your excuse?"

Collin Dodd stood up. "I'd like to address that. My uncle is the finest man I know. He'll make a fine mayor, and—"

"Sit down," Frances ordered. "You didn't have your hand raised, so you don't have the floor. Mr. Peterson?"

Ed Peterson stood up. "I've heard, *if* you're elected mayor, you plan to dam up Willow Creek, Dodd. Would you like to explain why, and what it would accomplish?"

Elmer's cheeks puffed out. "Don't know where you heard that, but it isn't true."

Norman Fuller opened his mouth, changed his mind, and raised a hand. When he got the okay from Frances, he spouted, "He heard it from me, Elmer, and if you remember, I thought it was a good idea, too. You said by damming up Willow Creek, more water will go into Sandhill Creek, make for better fishin', and we won't have the kind of floodin' we're having right now."

"And just where is Sandhill Creek?" Ed Peterson asked. "Unless I'm confusing it with some other creek, it runs right along

Elmer's dairy. I've also heard it's been dry for a good many years. Sounds to me like the only one to benefit from damming up Willow Creek would be Elmer Dodd."

Kathy Pressman held her baby to her shoulder and stood up. "I'd like to say something." When Fanny nodded, she went on. "My husband is a deputy sheriff. He works long, hard hours, and is underpaid. He drives a patrol car that's older than I am, and prays every day it doesn't break down, because there is no money in the town treasury to buy a replacement. *If* you become mayor, what are you going to do about that? The sheriff and his deputies are here to protect the town, yet they are treated like second-class citizens."

Elmer Dodd cleared his throat, and stumbled over his words. "Ah, well . . . That is . . . I, uh . . ."

Jennifer heard somebody say, "Do you suppose he knows what the sheriff's department is?"

Doc Chambers, a tall, thin man with a tuft of white hair and stooped shoulders, waved a hand. When he got the okay from Frances, he said, "I've got another question for Elmer Dodd, and it hasn't got anything to do with the sheriff's department or Willow Creek. *If* you're elected mayor, what do you plan to do about that plot of land you sold to the town for a ballpark? You know, the one you said had good drainage, and that's now sitting under four feet of water? You know, where the circus was set up a couple of weeks ago?"

Shocked, Jennifer didn't take the time to raise her hand before blurting out, "*You* sold that plot of land to the town for the ballpark? Elmer Dodd, is there no end to what you'll do to make a dollar?" She took a deep breath, and looked around the room. "In case you've all forgotten, Elmer Dodd was also responsible for giving that arid plot next to the dumps to the senior citizens so they could build the senior citizens' center, knowing full well it was crawling with underground fissures and streams, and wasn't fit for development. Well, in case you've forgotten, when a bad storm came through last year, that plot of land opened up with a dozen sinkholes, and the building that was under construction, collapsed. One man had a heart attack because of it. And in case you've forgotten, the senior citizens got a coalition together, sued Elmer, and Elmer settled out of court. And it was only then that the town council decided to give the senior citizens Calico Park to build their center."

Zeke Muller piped up. "And Willy Ashton represented the senior citizens in fine style. My vote is for Willy Ashton. He's a fine attorney, and he'll make a fine, honest mayor, who cares about the town and the people."

Norman Fuller responded with a snort. "Willy Ashton is just a kid. He's still wet behind the ears. His campaign is bein' funded with money from bake sales and car washes, for Pete's sake, and he don't know the first thing about runnin' a town."

Ken Hering stood up. "You're out of line, Mr. Fuller. Willy Ashton isn't here to defend himself, so you have no right to rag on him."

Elmer Dodd's dark eyes narrowed. "Whose side are you on, Hering?"

Ken returned, "Right is right and wrong is wrong, Dodd, and it isn't a matter of taking sides."

Charlie Waters jumped up. "You're a reporter for *The Calico Review*, Hering, and *The Calico Review* is backing Elmer Dodd. Where's your loyalty?"

Jack Boodie jumped up. "Shut up, Charlie. You're nothin' more than a creepy paperboy who manages to toss my paper in the mud every morning. You call it being a paper route driver, I call it being a creepy paperboy."

Charlie waters snapped back, "And you're nothing more than a lousy bartender, Jack Boodie. You own that crummy roadhouse and think you know it all."

When Charlie Waters and Jack Boodie went nose to nose, Fanny gave a shrill whistle for order, and the sheriff strode to the middle of the room. "That's enough!" he exclaimed. "You've all had your say, and we've listened. Now it's time to get to the real issues. Look around. We have people here who have lost their homes, and some still might. Our loyalty and concern belongs with them, and for each and every citizen who is going to be touched by this storm."

"Amen," Wes said, stepping forward. Peaches had her arms around his neck in a death grip, and he hugged her close. "And we can begin by saying a few prayers for Ron and Evie Kircher. Their jewelry store was robbed today." Gasps went up, but Wes went on. "That's right, so maybe you all best be thinking about them instead of the mayoral race. And about Norman Fuller, here, whose house is flooded out, or about the Cutlers, who lost their farm. I, for one, want to thank Frances and Fanny Cromwell for trying to bring some decorum to this unfortunate gathering, and I agree with Fanny. These good Calico residents need to be cheered up, not depressed, and we're going to begin right now. Elmer, you and your nephew are welcome to stay, but you'll have to park your politics outside the door."

Elmer muttered, "We have to be going. We're expected at the high school."

Ken Hering called out, "You might want to reconsider, Mr. Dodd. Willy Ashton is helping out at the high school tonight."

Collin followed his uncle to the door, and sneered over his shoulder, "Well, at least Ashton will be there to defend himself, won't he?"

When the door had closed firmly behind them, Frances spoke up. "Well, now, now, now that that unpleasantness is over, we're going to ask Pastor Wes to lead us in a few prayers, and then we're going to have a sing-along."

Nobody complained; nobody dared.

"Lordy, I didn't think we were ever going to get through the evening," Emma said, dropping wearily into a chair. "Those two ladies have more energy than twenty people half their age."

Emma, Wes, and Jennifer were sitting at the table in their bright yellow kitchen, drinking hot chocolate, and trying to wind down a little before going to bed. And thanks to the Cromwell sisters, Jennifer would be able to sleep in her own bed instead of on a cot with the animals in the Sunday-school room. It had been Fanny's idea, but Frances had heartily agreed. Peaches would have to spend the night in the makeshift kennel anyway, so the sisters volunteered to stay with the animals. The only problem had been trying to get Alice Cutler to join the evacuees in the social hall. But then she didn't want to spend the night with the sisters, either, and finally gave in.

Wes reached over and patted Emma's hand. "I know it's probably hard for you to admit, but those two ladies have been a big help. Might even consider them a godsend."

"And they are doing it out of the goodness of their hearts," Jennifer added. "Not because they are trying to impress us, or because they're out and about, trying to get votes."

Emma's eyes twinkled. "Well, after they took care of Elmer and Collin Dodd in such fine fashion, I guess I have to say they'd get my vote." Her eyes narrowed over Jennifer. "You seemed to be getting pretty chummy with that reporter, Jennifer. I don't want to poke my nose in where it doesn't belong, but . . ."

"Then best you keep your nose right in the middle of your face where it does belong," Wes teased.

"It's okay, Grandfather. I'm sure you're both a little confused. I mean, I'm the one who's been carrying on for the last year, calling Ken Hering arrogant and egotistical, and everything in between. And maybe he is, a little, but I don't think I've been fair. He really is quite nice, when you get to know him, and you heard how he stood up for Willy tonight. I thought it was remarkable. He spent the afternoon sandbagging, too, and. . . ." When Emma and Wes exchanged glances, a flush touched her cheeks. "All I meant to say is, I think we can consider him a friend."

Wes smiled. "Then that's good enough for me. Now, I'm going into my study to watch the weather report on the ten-o'clock news. And then I'm going to turn in. Morning is going to come mighty soon, and who knows what additional catastrophes the day will bring."

After Wes left the room, Emma shook her head. "He looks tired, but then I guess we all do. I didn't want to say anything while we were in the social hall, but does the sheriff have any clues about the robbery, or looting, as he calls it?"

"No, he doesn't. The door was unlocked, so it wasn't a forced entry. When that area was evacuated, the Kirchers were in such a hurry, they forgot to lock up. So either the culprit knew the door wasn't locked, or he went along the street trying door handles."

"In broad daylight? Lordy, that was pretty nervy."

"I know. And he only took small, expensive things. Like diamond rings and gold jewelry. Things he could stuff in his pockets, I would imagine. I was talking to Ken about it earlier, and he said he thinks the culprit is still in town, because Route 5 is closed in both directions. He also said he'd heard the Kirchers don't have any insurance, because they couldn't afford the premiums."

Emma sighed. "So many lives have been upended because of the storm."

"I know. . . ."

"Boy oh boy," Wes said, walking into the kitchen. "The weather report looks mighty favorable. Showers tomorrow, partial clearing the next day, and only blue skies after that."

Emma beamed. "Well, I'd say that calls for a plate of lemon wafers, and another cup of cocoa!"

"And a few dozen prayers of thanks," Wes said, giving Jennifer a hug. "I think I'll go over to the church, and give everybody the good news. They'll sleep a whole lot better, knowing the worst is over."

Emma gave a heartfelt sigh. "And so will we." She reached into the fruit bowl, and pulled out a banana. "Give this to Peaches, Wes, along with a big hug. And you tell the sisters not to worry. We'll get some of the senior citizens out to their cottage to fix the roof. It's the least we can do to repay them for their help and kindness."

Wes winked at Jennifer, and headed for the door.

Chapter Four

Jennifer had received the emergency call from Ben a little after five the next morning. The levee on the north side of White River Bridge was expected to give way at any time, and all the people who lived near the bridge were being evacuated, which included Penelope Davis and her fifteen cats.

Now, nearly two hours later, Jennifer and Ben stood in the middle of Penelope's cozy living room, listening to her rant and rave, and trying to make the woman understand the seriousness of the situation.

"I understand how you feel, Penelope,"

Ben said for the umpteenth time. "You don't want to leave your home and all your belongings, but as I see it, you don't have a choice. If that levee goes. . . ."

Penelope, a large, rawboned woman of Nordic extraction, waved her arms. "I've lived in this house for years, and I've seen many a storm, and that levee has held through each and every one of them. You can take my babies if you want, but I'm staying right here!"

Ben waved an arm in return. "Jennifer called her grandfather over an hour ago, Penelope, and he's expecting us. As a matter of fact, he's waiting to help unload the cats, so if you'll try to be reasonable. . . ."

Weary and agitated, Jennifer said firmly, "I think we've been patient long enough, Penelope. We had a lot of trouble rounding up that many cages and carrying cases, not to mention driving through nearly impassible roads to get to the clinic. And it was no easy task getting all the cats loaded into the cages and into our vehicles, either."

"I didn't ask for your help," Penelope

snapped. "It was the sheriff's doing. He's the one who's making a big deal out of this."

"Because it *is* a big deal," Jennifer replied. "We have several families who have lost their homes, but we've been very lucky, and so far nobody has lost their lives. If nothing else, think about your 'babies.' What will happen to them, if something happens to you? And think about how frightened they'll be at the church, without you there to give them comfort and love."

Tears welled up in Penelope's blue eyes. "Fluffy is afraid of strangers, and Smudge has to be hand-fed . . . You say you're keeping the animals in the Sunday-school room?"

"That's right, and you can stay right there with your babies, if you like."

"I'll have to take along some cat food . . ."

"That won't be necessary, Penelope. The feed and grain store donated a truckload of food and supplies, so we have as much as we need."

Penelope ran a hand through a tangle of silver-blond hair, and looked down at her wrinkled slacks. "I look a fright."

"Have you taken a good look at me?" Jennifer said gently. "Faded blue jeans, a grungy sweatshirt, and muddy shoes. And wait until you see the evacuees. Most of them are wearing donated clothes, and nobody cares. They are warm and dry, and that's all that matters."

Penelope sighed, and reached for her coat. "And I suppose Emma is in charge of things?"

Emma and Penelope went to school together, and in the years since, had never gotten along. Emma and Penelope had also gone to school with Frances Cromwell, and just the thought of the three of them in the same room together made Jennifer a little light-headed. Aware that if she so much as mentioned Frances's name, they would never get Penelope out of the house, and heaven only knew what would happen if she told the woman the Cromwell sisters had taken charge, Jennifer cleared her throat and said, "Emma is doing all she can to help, Penelope, just like everybody else."

Ben rolled his eyes, and opened the front door.

* * *

It was raining steadily by the time they reached the church and, at Wes's suggestion, they took the cats, and Penelope, in the back way, directly into the Sunday-school room.

"Sorry it took us so long," Jennifer said finally, kissing Wes's cheek, "but we ran into some problems."

"Uh-huh, well, we've had a few problems here, too," Wes said, forcing a smile for Penelope's benefit. "I'm sure you're feeling a bit put out by this, Penelope, but I truly believe if we can get through the next forty-eight hours, the worst will be over."

Penelope sniffed. "Well, I hope and pray you're right. Jennifer said I can stay in here with my babies, and that's what I'm going to do. Don't feel exactly sociable at the moment, and I'm not in the best temper." She gave a big sigh. "So many dogs. . . . Dear, oh dear, I hope they all don't start barking at once. My babies will get so upset, and then—" She gasped, and pointed. "My word, what is *that*!"

Jennifer looked over at the turkey platter full of banana skins, grape stalks, and orange rinds, and knew exactly what it was: Peaches's breakfast. She glanced at Wes, but all he did was give her a helpless shrug. "Ah, well, that looks like Emma's turkey platter, and what's left of the chimp's breakfast."

Penelope's brows drew together in a scowl. "Chimp?" And then her face reddened. "Chimp. You mean like in chimpanzee? I've heard all about the crazy Cromwell sisters and that chimpanzee they got from the circus. I've heard all about them parading her all over town, dressed up like a Barbie doll, so if that pile of banana skins means . . ."

"It means Peaches has her tummy full, and now it's time to fill ours," Fanny announced, stomping into the room. "Breakfast is ready, so you'd better come get it while it's hot." She glowered at Penelope. "We had to hold up breakfast because of you, Penelope Davis. I told Frances you were probably taking your sweet time, putting on your makeup, curling your hair, and ironing your dress." She peered over her granny glasses. "Well, if you were doing all that, it didn't help much." She pointed at her pocket watch, hanging from the chain around her waist. "Frances told me to keep my watch handy. Everything has to run nice and smooth, and on time. Well, it's almost eight o'clock, and those good folks in there have waited for breakfast long enough. Frances said to tell you there's plenty of food, if you have a mind to eat."

Penelope looked like she might faint, and muttered, "I'm staying right here."

"Suit yourself," Fanny said, marching off.

"I'll stay with Penelope," Ben said, trying for a smile.

Jennifer said, "You should eat, Ben."

"If you'll dish me up a plate, I'll nuke it in the microwave later."

"Consider it done," Jennifer said, concluding that Ben Copeland had to be the bravest man alive to offer to stay with the disagreeable woman, who now had tears streaming down her cheeks.

"So, I gather the problems you were talking about have to do with the Cromwell sisters?" Jennifer asked when they were out of earshot.

Wes sighed. "Partly. They had a fit when

they found out Penelope was coming here with her fifteen cats. But the trouble started long before that. Guess you could say it started the minute Emma found out the sisters planned to cook breakfast. They said it was the *least* they could do. Well, you know Emma feels that the kitchen, here and at home, is her domain. But the sisters weren't taking no for an answer. Emma finally gave up, but she's still talking to herself, so you know she must be pretty upset. And I dread what's going to happen when she sees the kitchen. I don't think a tornado could've made a bigger mess. Then Norman Fuller got into a hassle with Doc Chambers, and walked out. Said he was going to the high school, because anything had to be better than staying here. Oh, and the Pressmans went home. Manny found a way around the flooded road. Millie Perkins and Fanny are still trying to outdo each other in the one-upmanship department, Fred Perkins looks like he's lost his last friend, and Alice Cutler looks like she's about to die. About the only plus is the fact that nobody is arguing. But then, nobody is speaking to each other, either."

"Do you think Alice Cutler is seriously ill?" Jennifer asked.

"I don't think it's physical, sweetheart. She's distressed over the loss of her home, and who can blame her? Oh, and Willy stopped by. He just wanted to touch base. He looks about as good as the rest of us, and that isn't saying much."

"Did he say anything about Elmer Dodd?"

"You mean, did Elmer show up at the high school last night? I asked him, and no, Elmer didn't. Maybe he was afraid to, after the reception he got here."

They'd reached the social hall, and Jennifer braced herself. Wes had said if they got through the next forty-eight hours, the worst would be over, but at the moment, forty-eight hours seemed like several light-years away.

Somebody had opened up the drapes, letting in the gray, dismal day, and although a fire was still burning in the potbellied stove, the room seemed cold and damp. And it was definitely full of gloomy faces. Emma was stacking blocks with Peaches at a table in the corner, and although she smiled at Jennifer, the smile didn't reach her eyes. And both Millie and Fred looked glum, too. The only cheerfulness in the room came from Frances and Fanny, who chattered like magpies while they set up the breakfast buffet, and then insisted Jennifer and Wes try a little bit of everything. And what a buffet it was! Stacks of pancakes with Fanny's strawberry jam, platters of scrambled eggs, mounds of sausage patties, bowls of cream gravy, corn bread, apple bread, and nut bread, and tall pitchers of apple juice. Jennifer nearly swooned, counting the calories, but she was too hungry to make a final tally. And like her grandfather was always saying, there were just some times when a body needed comfort food, and this was definitely one of them.

Slowly, the evacuees made their way to the table, like the *last* thing on their minds was food, and it occurred to Jennifer that everything about them was mechanical. Even lifting their forks to their mouths. Not wanting to sit with any of them because it was all too depressing, Jennifer and Wes joined Emma and Peaches. Peaches was sitting at the table like a big girl, playing with her colorful blocks, and when she looked up at Jennifer and Wes, she gurgled, and pulled her gums back over her teeth. It was her way of smiling, and it was very endearing.

"You want me to dish up a plate for you?" Wes asked Emma.

Emma looked at his plate of food, and wrinkled her nose. "I'll get something later. So, is Penelope all set up in the Sunday-school room?"

"She is, and I have the feeling that's where she's going to stay," Jennifer said, winking at Peaches. Peaches winked back. She was also eyeing the apple juice. Normally, Jennifer would have given her a sip, but not knowing what kind of liquid surprises the sisters might have put in the concoction, Jennifer thought she'd better try it, first. One sip, and then two. By the third sip, she knew it contained something besides apple juice, and shook her head. "Sorry, sweetie, but we'd better not."

Wes took a sip, and grinned. "I don't think

it's hooch, sweetheart, if that's what you're worried about, but I'll admit, it's different."

Horrified, Emma exclaimed, "Hooch! Are you telling me those nutty sisters brought moonshine into the church?"

Wes admonished, "Keep your voice down, Emma, before you start a riot. I wouldn't put it past them, but this isn't moonshine. It's interesting, but I think it's perfectly harmless."

Emma took a sip, and frowned. "I wouldn't be too sure. Tastes like spoiled apples to me." She took another sip. "I think I taste cloves and cinnamon, too."

Jennifer laughed. "Well, without a chemist's analysis, I'm not about to give it to Peaches."

A few minutes later, Ben walked into the room, dished up, and joined them. "Couldn't handle it any longer," he said, taking a sip of juice. "Penelope is on a crying jag, and all the dogs are howling." He took another sip. "Not bad. Tastes a little like Irene's apple pie when the apples are too ripe." He looked out at the rain, and shook his head. "We could sure use a break in the weather."

"How was it out at the clinic this morning?" Wes asked.

"Treacherous going. We were up to our hubcaps in several spots, but I don't think we have to worry about the clinic. And the last I heard, they've got the Front Street levee under control."

Wes chewed on a bit of sausage, and beamed with pleasure. "This doesn't taste like sausage, either, but it's mighty good." He offered a bite to Emma, and waited.

"Hmm. Well, it's not bad." She looked around for the sisters, didn't see them, and stood up. "Well, guess I might as well fix me a small plate."

Peaches pulled back her lips, and smiled.

Wes smiled, too. "Figured you'd change your mind, sooner or later."

It took Emma only a moment to dish up, and she had no sooner gotten back to the table when the sheriff walked in with two young, bedraggled couples. Jennifer didn't recognize them, but with so many new people moving into town every day, it was impossible to keep track.

"Well, now," the sheriff said. "Looks like I

got these youngsters here at the right time. A hearty breakfast, and they'll feel a lot better. This is Bob Smith, Jane Brown, Tom Davis, and Patty Jones. They were camping along Willow Creek, and barely got out with the clothes on their backs before the flood water took out their campsite. Had to leave everything behind, including their van that's now stuck in the mud. Found them down on the highway, trying to thumb a ride into town. Kids, this is Jennifer Gray and Ben Copeland, our resident veterinarians. This pretty lady is Emma Morrison, and the man with the white hair is Wes Gray, our kindly pastor. And that little critter with the strange smile is Peaches." He looked around. "Don't suppose there is much point in introducing you to anybody else. Whoa, what a bunch of down faces. Well, you'll all be happy to know the storm is breaking in the south. I have the feeling in a couple of hours, we might even see some blue sky."

While the sheriff went on, giving them an update about the levees and streets that were still flooded, Jennifer studied the foursome. They all looked like they were in their early twenties, and didn't seem to be too friendly. Darting eyes, a lot of fidgeting, and the tall, thin young man named Tom kept biting at his bottom lip. Patty, who was very tiny and very, very pale, carried a knapsack over her back, and wouldn't look anybody in the eye. Not even when Jennifer addressed her directly. "You look frozen clear through, Patty. Why don't you leave your knapsack here, and dish up breakfast? There's plenty of food, and the coffee is hot . . ."

"We ate already," Patty said, looking up at Tom with frightened eyes.

Jane snapped her gum, and shrugged. "Well, I'd like something to eat."

"Me, too," Bob said, heading for the buffet table.

"If it's okay, we'll just stand by the fire for a while," Tom said, putting a protective arm around Patty.

"Well, that's a strange foursome," Jennifer said after they'd moved off.

The sheriff returned, "Yeah, well, I thought so, too, until I considered what they've just been through. One minute they were out camping, having a good old time, and the next minute they were under water. Had to be a bit scary."

"Did they say where they're from?" Jennifer asked.

"Uh-huh. Council Bluffs. College kids with some time on their hands to dawdle away the summer."

"Did you see the van?"

"Nope. They drove along the creek quite a ways before they found a good spot to camp. Didn't have the heart to tell them they were supposed to get a permit. I made arrangements to have the van towed in, but like everything else, it's gonna take time. Grundy says they're backlogged for days. They are just now getting to the Perkinses' vehicle. Which brings to mind something else. For all the people who have lost their homes, or can't go home for whatever reason, Rose Kelly at the boardinghouse has a few vacant rooms. Talked to Walt Jensen at the hotel, too, and he can put a few people up. Same with the motel out near the mall. The shelters are serving a purpose, but these people need a place to stay that they can call home, until the repairs and rebuilding is done. Mayor Attwater has talked to the governor, and we're gonna get some funding. But that's gonna take time, too."

Wes shook his head. "It's a sad time for everybody, Jim. Do you have a final tally on the displaced families?"

"Twelve, and I think we can be thankful there aren't more. Three farms lost, but the rest of it is water damage, leaky roofs, flooded basements, that sort of thing."

"What about Nettie Balkin and Norman Fuller?"

"Flooded basements and water damage. They were lucky. I don't see Fuller. I wanted to give him the good news."

Emma clucked her tongue. "You'll find him at the high school. Said he didn't like our company. I'm beginning to think Millie and Fred Perkins feel the same way. They were so friendly in the beginning, and now look at them. If you want my opinion, I think they've had some kind of a tiff."

The sheriff sighed. "They look like everybody else. Like robots, going through the motions. Well, what do you make of that?"

The sheriff was referring to the two young

couples, who were now huddled against the far wall, arguing. Jennifer couldn't hear their words, but she could see the body language. Flailing arms, scowling faces. And Patty was crying.

"Boy oh boy," Wes said. "Best we stay out of it, but that looks like one unhappy young lady to me."

Suddenly, Patty stalked off, sat down on the floor in the corner, and buried her head in her arms.

Emma said, "Lordy, the poor little thing. Wes, maybe you should talk to her."

"Not yet, Emma. Let's see if they can work it out. Like Jim said, they've been through a lot, and now they're stranded in a strange town. Any word when Route 5 is going to open up?"

"If the weather breaks, in a day or two, I would imagine. Road crew is working on it now, digging ditches for drainage. If you don't mind, Emma, I think I'll dish up a little bit of your fine cooking. Everybody seems to have cleaned their plates, at least at this table, and that tells me I'm in for a treat."

Emma snorted, "Good or bad, I can't take

the credit. The Cromwell sisters took over the kitchen, just like they've taken over everything else. They cooked the food."

The sheriff looked at the dregs in their juice glasses, and frowned. "Does that include the juice?"

Wes chuckled. "That includes the juice. Be sure to try some, Jim. You won't regret it."

"Somebody should fix Penelope a plate, and see that she eats every morsel," Jennifer said.

Emma gave a loud harrumph. "Well, don't look at me! She'd probably accuse me of lacing everything with poison."

"I'll do it," Wes said. "If I try hard enough, I might even get her to smile."

Ben looked at his watch. "Guess I'd better go. Irene is going to think I've fallen in the river. I'll be back in time to feed and exercise the animals, Jennifer. Can't expect you to do it all alone."

"Stay home, and give your wife a reason to smile," Wes said. "The sisters took care of the animals last night, and quite admirably, I might add, and we're all capable of giving Jennifer a helping hand."

Jennifer gave Ben a hug. "Grandfather is right, Ben. If I need you for anything, I'll call. Promise. Now, if you'll excuse me, I'm going to go talk to Millie and Fred, and see if I can find where they've hidden those wonderful smiles."

Millie looked up, but didn't smile, as Jennifer approached their table, and Jennifer's heart gave a little twist. Had they had a serious argument? Fred looked up, too, with lifeless eyes. "Ah, Jennifer," he said, heaving a sigh. "You can keep my wife company, while I take Tootsie Marie for a walk. Gotta get some air."

"Is he okay?" Jennifer asked, after Fred had gone.

Tears filled the woman's eyes. "I don't know, Jennifer, I truly don't. He had a terrible night last night, and was up more than he was down."

Jennifer patted Millie's hand. "Well, sleeping on a cot in a room filled with strangers can't be very pleasant."

"No, it isn't, but I don't think it's that. I don't think he's feeling well." She motioned toward his plate. "He hardly touched breakfast, and I can see something in his eyes. It's like he's in pain. Worse, when I broached the subject, he got very angry. That's not like him either." She sighed. "So much sadness. Like that young girl over in the corner. She looks so unhappy. I figured she must've had a fight with her boyfriend, because he looks pretty miserable, too. So many sad stories to tell. Were they flooded out?"

"They aren't locals, Millie. They were camping along Willow Creek, and got caught in the flood. Had to leave everything behind, including their van."

"Well, that certainly explains their behavior."

Just then, a thunderous crash sounded in the kitchen, and loud voices followed. "Oh-oh," Jennifer said. "Something tells me the cooks have gotten into a skirmish, and I'd better intervene. If you'll excuse me . . ."

Finally, a smile played at the corners of Millie's mouth. "Those two sisters are something else, that's for sure. While you're in the kitchen, maybe you can ask them what they put in the apple juice? I've never tasted anything like it, and would surely like to have the recipe. I'd ask them myself, but they're a bit intimidating, if you know what I mean."

Jennifer smiled, and headed for the kitchen.

Jennifer stared around the kitchen in amazement. It was clean. No, it was beyond clean. It was spotless, and the sisters had even mopped the floor.

Frances looked at Fanny, and scowled. "Now you've done it, sister. Your temper tantrum and bellyaching has brought little Jennifer Gray right in, to see what's going on. Next, we'll have Emma on the warpath, and then Penelope Davis, accusing us of waking up her four hundred and forty cats."

Fanny poked a finger at her sister. "Don't you be blamin' me for your shortcomings, sister. You're the one who started it. Well, it don't matter none. Little Jennifer Gray can see we ain't killed each other, and the feudin' is over." She smiled at Jennifer. "Did everybody get enough to eat?"

"Yes, and everything was wonderful. Especially the apple juice. Quite a few people would like to know what you put in it, besides apple juice."

Fanny's eyes twinkled. "Can't tell ya. That's my secret. Won't even let Frances around when I'm makin' it. Got that recipe from Uncle Mitford when I was just a little tyke about that high." She waved a hand.

"And your uncle wouldn't tell Frances?"

Frances sucked in her cheeks. "Fanny was Uncle Mitford's favorite, and they had a lot of secrets. Well, I was our daddy's favorite, and we had us some secrets, too, and I still have 'em. Like the sausage. That's *my* recipe, and Fanny don't have any idea what goes into it."

"I'll bet I know," Jennifer said, giving them her sweetest smile. "I'll bet you put your wonderful elixir in everything, including the juice and the sausage."

Pleased, Fanny's face lit up. "You hear that, Sister? I told you that's what they'd think. Well, I don't know about Frances, but I didn't use one drop of elixir in the apple juice, but I take your comment as a compliment."

Frances shook her head. "Didn't put one

drop in the sausage, either. Best we get to cleaning up in the other room, Sister. Before we know it, it'll be time to fix supper." Her eyes twinkled, too. "Fanny is cooking one half, and I'm cooking the other. Like I said, she's got her secrets, and I've got mine, but nobody is going to mind a few secrets, or a few surprises."

Jennifer couldn't imagine, and didn't dare ask.

Chapter Five

"Your grandfather said I'd probably find you sitting in the sun," Ken Hering said, climbing the porch steps of the Gray house a little hesitantly. "Well, I sure don't want to bother you, or interrupt anything, but . . . Well . . ."

He looked so uncomfortable, Jennifer couldn't help but smile. "You're not interrupting anything, Ken. Now that the rain has stopped, most of the evacuees have gone home to assess the damage and make other plans if, in fact, they can't stay in their houses. So I suddenly found myself with some free time, and wanted to take advantage of the sun."

"I heard about the arrangements being made for the evacuees whose homes are uninhabitable. Guess staying in a hotel room or at the boardinghouse would be better than sleeping on the floor in the church or in the high school gymnasium. What about the Cutlers?"

"They left about an hour ago with Charlie and Margie Waters. The Waterses will be putting them up for a while."

"Did they take Bosworth?"

"They did. We managed to reunite the rest of the animals with their owners today, so all we have left, not counting the Perkinses' Yorkie and the chimp, are Penelope Davis's cats."

"And you might not have them after tomorrow morning," Ken said. "I've heard the White River Bridge levee is holding, so I would imagine the evacuees from that area can go home before too long."

Ken sat down in the wrought-iron chair beside Jennifer, and looked around. "It's nice here. Peaceful."

"Yes, it is, and the sun feels wonderful. We spend a lot of time on the porch during the summer months, especially in the evenings. I wish you could see the garden the way it's supposed to look. Grandfather grows the vegetables, and Emma grows the flowers, and now everything is lost. By the time the ground dries out enough to replant, it will be too late in the season to start over. I know, that seems rather insignificant compared to all the horrible things that have happened to the town, but it still makes me sad. You're not carrying your camera."

"I left it in the car. I didn't come here to take pictures. I just wanted to see how everybody is doing." He gave her a lopsided grin. "When I left the social hall, Penelope Davis and Fanny Cromwell were going round and round about how to make gravy without lumps, Emma was sparring with Frances, and your grandfather was trying to teach the chimp to play checkers."

"What about the kids?"

"The foursome who were camping along Willow Creek? Your grandfather told me about them. I tried to interview them, but they weren't having any of that. The tall dude actually got hostile. It struck me as a rather odd way to behave, in light of their predicament. I mean, you'd think they'd show a little appreciation. They have a place to stay and free food, so what more do they want?"

"Is the girl with the blond hair still sitting off by herself?"

"If you're talking about the girl who breaks out in tears every few minutes, and keeps clutching her knapsack like it's her lifeline, yes and no. She isn't hanging with her friends, if that's what you mean, but Millie Perkins seems to have gained her confidence. When I left, Millie was talking, and the girl was listening. Couldn't hear what Millie was saying, but things looked pretty intense."

"And Fred Perkins?"

"Glum and antisocial. As I recall, he was in fairly good spirits last night. Of course, that was before he had to spend the night on a cot with a roomful of strangers. I was glad to hear their car made it through the mud bath, but for some cleanup and minor repairs. Sounds like by the time Route 5 opens up, they can be on their way to Omaha. Did you see the newspaper this morning?"

"No, I didn't. Ben and I were up at dawn, trying to round up enough carrying cases and cages for Penelope's cats. She didn't want to leave, which proved to be a bigger problem than transporting her cats."

"Well, I don't expect to get a Pulitzer or anything, but all those shots I took yesterday turned out pretty good. John, Jr., ran a collage on the front page. Tomorrow, we'll be covering the mayor's ordeal."

"What happened to Mayor Attwater?"

"He ran his car into the front of Fenten's Ice Cream Parlor. He was making the turn onto Park Lane, hit a puddle, and lost control."

"Oh, no!"

"And if that wasn't bad enough, old man Fenten was inside, and got pinned up against the frosty machine. No injuries, just a lot of shot nerves and angry words, and the last I heard, Fenten is going to sue Attwater for every penny he has."

Jennifer looked at him slyly. "And I suppose you were right there with your camera?"

"Hey, what can I say? I'm a reporter, and it's my job to stay on top of things, even if I don't always get all the answers. For example, I'd still like to know where you found the camel. For days, John, Jr., gave the missing camel front-page coverage. *'Carousing Camel Canters Away from The Cannon Family Circus.'* Everybody in Calico was looking for him, and then all of a sudden, we heard you'd found him. Not how, or where, you understand. Just that you'd found him, and that the camel had been returned to the circus, and everybody was happy. So, the circus leaves town, and the next thing we know, the Cromwell sisters have the chimp. The same chimp, I might add, that caused one truckload of trouble for the circus on opening night. So what's the story, Jennifer? Is there a connection? And why all the secrecy?"

"I'll never tell. By the way, I'd like to thank you for standing up for Willy last night."

Ken shrugged. "Like I said, nobody has

the right to criticize somebody who isn't around to defend himself. John, Jr., says you went to school with Willy, and you're just good friends. Is that true?"

Jennifer sighed. "You're not going to give up, are you? Yes, Willy and I went to school together. And we *are* good friends."

"*Just* good friends?"

"Are you asking me if we're romantically involved? No, not really. We're good friends. We have a good time together, but we're much too busy with our careers to get serious about each other."

"That sounds boring, but encouraging." His green eyes flickered over her. "So, if I were to ask you for a date, Willy wouldn't object?"

"Willy probably wouldn't object, but I might. Look, Ken, up until yesterday, I had you in the same category with John Wexler, Jr. Arrogant and egotistical."

He smiled. "Means the same thing."

"No, it doesn't. In my book, arrogant means insolent, and egotistical means conceited."

The smile widened. "So what happened yesterday to change your mind?"

"I saw a side of you I hadn't seen before. A caring side, that makes me wonder what's really under all that pushy arrogance."

"So, have you figured it out?"

"No, I haven't, nor have I had the time, or the inclination. If that sounds a little arrogant on my part, I'm sorry. But you have to understand where I'm coming from. You can't dislike someone one day, and like him the next. It's more complicated than that, and I don't have time for complications in my life."

"Well, I'm a patient man," he said easily. "And I haven't met a complication yet that can't be worked out. Guess I'd better warn you. I can also be persistent and tenacious."

"Means the same thing," Jennifer said, trying to hold back her smile.

"No way. Persistent means I don't give up easily. Tenacious means I'm like a dog with a bone. I won't give it up without a fight."

"Still means the same thing."

He gave her a toothpaste-ad grin. "Is that a smile I see tugging at the corners of your mouth? It's good to see you smile, Jennifer. Heaven knows, we need a lot more of it. The whole town needs to smile again."

Relieved to see her grandfather making his way along the pathway, Jennifer took a deep breath. Without a doubt, Ken Hering was still the most maddening man she'd ever met.

Wes nodded at Ken. "Told you you'd find her sitting in the sun. Must say, the sun feels mighty good, and seeing all that blue sky is a true pleasure." He gave Jennifer an apologetic smile. "Sorry for the interruption, sweetheart, but the sheriff called. Somebody spotted a stray dog near the junction of Route 5 and Marshton Road. Looked to be in pretty bad shape, so he thought you'd want to handle it."

"I'll take you," Ken said, getting to his feet. "I have a Ford Bronco. It's tough and tenacious, like me."

"Ulterior motive?" Jennifer asked.

"Caught me. I'd like to take some pictures, if you don't mind."

Jennifer didn't mind, nor did she mind

that he was going to take her, and it was a fact she found more than disconcerting.

"Now what?" Ken asked, pulling the Bronco off to the side of the road.

Jennifer sighed. "I don't know, Ken. We've been at it a good hour, and we've looked everywhere, so I think about all we can do now is hope the dog found its way home."

"Or hope it didn't get stuck in the mud along Willow Creek. Shall we head back to town?"

"Willow Creek."

"Beg pardon?"

"Willow Creek. Do you mind taking a little side trip first?"

He gave her a broad wink. "What do you have in mind?"

"Silly. Nothing romantic, I can assure you. I'd like to take a look at those stranded kids' van."

"Willow Creek goes on for miles, Jennifer. Clear into Cherry County, and it'll be tough going at best. I wouldn't want to be out in the middle of nowhere after dark, not even in my trusty four-wheel-drive."

"We still have a couple of hours of daylight," Jennifer pressed. "I'll make a deal with you. We'll go look for the van, and if we haven't found it in an hour, we'll head back."

"Then we'd better take to the high ground on the east side of Willow Creek," Ken said, turning the Bronco around. "You want to tell me what this is all about?"

"Off the record?"

"You're not talking to a newspaper reporter now, Jennifer. You're talking to a friend."

"Fair enough, but to tell you the truth, I don't know why I want to see the van. Maybe I just want to prove to myself there is one, and that the kids were actually camped along Willow Creek when the storm hit. Or maybe I want to find something to justify their odd behavior, and the fact they have names like Smith, Brown, and Jones."

Ken frowned. "Say what?"

"Bob Smith, Jane Brown, Tom Davis, and Patty Jones. Don't those names sound kind of phony to you?"

"Maybe, but they are also common names. Open up any phone book in Anytown,

U.S.A., and you'll find dozens of each. Did the sheriff ask them for identification?"

"I doubt it. Why would he? The kids said they were camping along Willow Creek, and their van got stuck in the mud. The sheriff is a very compassionate man, and I'm sure he felt sorry for them."

Ken frowned. "The sheriff just had a jewelry store robbery, too, so wouldn't you think he'd want to I.D. every stranger he came in contact with?"

Jennifer sighed. "Look around, Ken. Calico is growing in leaps and bounds. Walk down the street on any given day of the week, and you'll be lucky to see a familiar face. And I'm not suggesting the kids robbed the jewelry store. I'm simply suggesting they're acting strangely, and they might not be who they say they are."

"Escaped convicts from Attica?" Ken teased. "Or maybe direct descendants of Bonnie and Clyde, out on a crime spree?"

"I wouldn't expect you to take this seriously, but humor me? If it weren't for Patty, the blond girl who seems so miserable, and their fidgety, nervous behavior, I probably wouldn't be giving it a second thought."

"Uh-huh, so they kidnapped the blonde, and were keeping her in the back of the van when the storm hit. And under those plaid shirts, they are all carrying Dirty Harry longslides."

"You have a vivid imagination."

"I'm a reporter, remember?"

"Uh-huh, and like John, Jr., if there isn't a story, you'll create one."

Ken grunted. "Not me. That's John, Jr.'s, little trick. He calls it cleaver journalism, and I call it bad fiction."

Surprised, but pleased, Jennifer said, "So, when are you going to get a byline so you can show John, Jr., how it's supposed to be done?"

"I'm working on it, and thanks for the vote of confidence."

They were driving along the east side of Willow Creek now, where there hadn't been any flooding, but the ground was still a marshy goo. In several spots, Ken had to gun the motor to make it through, and a couple of times the Bronco fishtailed.

When they came to a cross stream filled with boulders and debris, Jennifer shook her head. “I think this was a mistake, Ken. We’d better go back.”

“No way. Your hunch was correct. Look off to your right. No, more to your right, near that stand of cottonwoods.”

“It’s the van!” Jennifer exclaimed.

“Uh-huh, and we’re going through. Hang on.”

Jennifer hung on, and closed her eyes. When the jostling and bumping stopped, she opened them, and took a ragged breath. “That was some driving.”

Ken smiled. “You ought to see me drive through sleet and snow.”

Ken stopped the Bronco on a little rise overlooking the mud hole where the van was bogged down, and said, “Now I suppose you want to get a closer look?”

“I don’t think we can, Ken. We’ll sink up to our hips in the mud.”

“Not if we go in the way the kids came out. See the log propped up between the bank and the rocks near the open door? Are you any good at walking across slippery logs?”

"Not too good, I'm afraid," Jennifer muttered. "And I sure don't like the idea of falling face first in the mud."

Ken grinned. "I'll go first. If you chicken out, I won't tell anybody."

"You're not wearing boots, Ken, so I don't—"

He cut her off with a wave of his hand. "You think I drive around unprepared? I have boots in the back, and just about everything else I might need for any situation. Even a fishing pole, a shotgun, and a pair of binoculars."

"Well, I won't ask you what all that is for," Jennifer said, making her way down the muddy embankment.

Ken caught up with Jennifer by the time she reached the log, but after a closer inspection, he didn't have to talk her into staying on the bank. While Ken tightrope-walked across, using his arms for balance, Jennifer studied the surrounding area, but could see no signs of a camp.

When Ken reached the van, she called out, "I don't think they camped here."

"Maybe they were camping in the van."

He gave her a thumbs-up, and climbed in through the open door.

"It's been stripped," he said when he reappeared a few minutes later.

"Stripped?" Jennifer asked incredulously.

"Stripped. No vehicle registration or insurance papers, or any of the stuff you normally find in a glove box. Not even a candy wrapper. And no personal belongings. From where you're standing, can you see the rear license plate?"

Jennifer moved down the bank a few feet, and shook her head. "There isn't one."

"Now, why isn't that a surprise? And five cents will get you a stick of chewing gum that there isn't a front plate, either." He made his way across the log, and ran a hand through his red hair. "Bet it's a stolen vehicle, and the kids stripped it themselves. I don't know about you, but I think we should have a little talk with the sheriff."

Jennifer shivered, remembering Ken's comment: *"And under those plaid shirts, they are all carrying Dirty Harry longslides."*

Ken gave her an easy smile. "Relax, Jennifer. We'll get to the bottom of it, and if it will make you feel better, I don't think they're dangerous. Misguided, maybe, and they *are* probably on the run, but that doesn't make them 'America's Most Wanted.' "

Jennifer wanted to take comfort in his words, but she couldn't. And it was all she could do to smile when he said, "I think I finally know what makes you tick, Jennifer Gray. You might be shivering, and even showing signs of anxiety, but I can see the excitement in your eyes. You like a good mystery, just as much as I do. You'd make a good reporter, and that was meant to be a compliment." He looked at his watch. "It's almost six. Do you think the sheriff is still in his office?"

"No, I don't, but he's supposed to be dropping by the church later. We can talk to him them, unless you have other plans, and can't wait."

"I have nothing but time," Ken said, leading the way up the embankment.

"Good! Then you can join us for supper."

"Two nights in a row. I'm flattered."

"Well, you might not feel that way after

you've tasted the food. Last night, we had Emma's terrific lasagna. Tonight, we're having Frances and Fanny Cromwell's 'secret surprises.' "

"Can't cook, huh?"

"Oh, they can cook, but their dishes are chock-full of secret ingredients, guaranteed to grow hair on a bald man's head."

Ken threw his head back and laughed. "Eye of newt and butterfly wings?"

"Uh-huh, and those are just the seasonings."

Ken turned around to help Jennifer over a fallen log, and winked. "Along with everything else, I'm also a man who likes a good challenge."

"Lordy, am I glad to see you," Emma said, giving Jennifer a hug. "Maybe those crazy sisters will listen to you. I've been trying to tell them for the last two hours they're cooking up too much food. All we have left, besides us, are those four kids, the Perkinses, and Penelope Davis." She looked up at Ken, and frowned. "Unless you're staying."

"I wouldn't miss it," Ken said, giving

Emma a warm smile. "Though just between you and me, I'd rather be eating your terrific lasagna instead of the Cromwell sisters' 'secret surprises.' "

Emma flushed. "Hmm, well, I guess I should consider that a compliment."

Jennifer replied, "Yes, you should, Emma, though whatever they're cooking sure smells good."

Emma harrumphed. "Smells like crispy-fried polecat to me. Did you find the dog?"

"No, we didn't," Jennifer said, "but we found something else. Is Grandfather around?"

"He's in his office with Fred Perkins. They've been in there a good hour with the door closed, so I have no idea what's going on. Millie doesn't know, either, and it's bothering her. But she doesn't seem to be dwelling on it. She's taken little Patty under her wing, and has hardly left her side."

"And the other three?"

"They've been out in the courtyard arguing for the last hour. Before they went out, I heard the gist of it. Bob and Jane want to leave the van and hike to the next town, but

Patty won't leave, and Tom doesn't want to leave Patty. Of course, you have to understand all that wasn't meant for my ears, so I could've gotten some of it mixed up."

"I doubt that," Jennifer said, looking around. "Because you have super hearing. Is Penelope with her cats?"

"She is, and Peaches is with your granddaddy and Fred." Her eyes narrowed over Jennifer. "I know that look, young lady. You said you found something, and want to talk to your granddaddy, so that tells me we have another mystery afoot."

Jennifer lowered her voice. "We found the van, Emma, but it was stripped clean. No registration or personal belongings, and even the license plates were gone."

Emma frowned. "Well, that's a strange one. Why would somebody want to do a thing like that?"

"To keep the sheriff from finding out it's a stolen vehicle," Ken said. "I think the kids stripped it themselves, Emma, and what you said about the kids wanting to leave the van and hike to the next town, simply supports my theory."

Jennifer said, "And what about their names, Emma? Smith, Brown, Davis, and Jones? Sounds like four aliases to me."

Emma sighed. "Lordy, what next? Do you suppose the sheriff asked them for identification?"

Jennifer shook her head. "No, but I think it's about time he did. I'd also like to know what Patty has in that knapsack she's been guarding so faithfully."

Emma clucked her tongue. "All that stuff they took out of the van, along with the license plates, would be my guess. Hmm. If they could steal a vehicle, do you suppose they are capable of robbing a jewelry store?"

"The thought occurred to me," Jennifer replied, "but if they *are* the culprits, why did the sheriff find them hitchhiking *into* town? I mean, wouldn't they want to get away from town as quickly as possible?"

"Try this little scenario," Ken said. "They steal a van somewhere, and decide to take all the back roads through Nebraska. For whatever reason, they camp along Willow Creek, and along comes the storm. The van gets stuck in the mud, so they have to leave it, but strip it first, which would make it a lot harder for the law to identify it as a stolen vehicle, in the event there is a B.O.L.O."

Emma raised a brow. "What's a B.O.L.O.?".

"Be on the Lookout. So now they're on the highway, headed out of town, and along comes the sheriff. They find out Route 5 is closed in both directions, which means there isn't any through traffic, either, which also means the sheriff isn't going to buy their story, because there is no logical reason for them to be there. So they decide to tell him the truth. But they don't say anything about the van being stripped, because when the time comes, they plan to play dumb. Like, somebody else must have come along after they left it, and stripped it. They know the sheriff is going to make arrangements to have the van towed in, and that's cool. All they have to do is wait it out. By the time the road opens, they'll have the van, and it's adios. But the whole thing has them a bit nervous, and fidgety. The longer they stick around, the better chance there is of getting caught. And when they find out getting the van is going to take a lot longer than they thought—and right about now, time is their enemy—Bob and Jane decide the best thing to do is hitchhike to the next town, and forget about the van. Maybe they figure they can steal another set of wheels later on. Some other town, some other day. But for some reason, Patty doesn't want to leave, and Tom doesn't want to leave Patty. How am I doing so far?"

Jennifer said, "It sounds plausible, but why doesn't Patty want to leave? And why is she acting like her friends are her enemies?"

Emma pursed her lips. "Maybe they'd already been to town when the sheriff found them. They stripped the van and left it when it bogged down in the mud, and came to town for the sole purpose of getting their hands on some money. They robbed the jewelry store, and were on their way out of town when the sheriff found them. But when they found out Route 5 was closed, they had to change their plans. So how am *I* doing?"

Ken grinned. "You know, she's really

good, Jennifer. No wonder you think like a sleuth. You've had a good teacher."

"Emma thinks like a sleuth because she reads mystery novels by the dozens, Ken."

"No kidding? Do you like Presten Campbell?"

Emma beamed. "I do. Just finished *Dead on the Beach,* but I knew who the killer was before I got to page ten."

Jennifer tossed up her hands in defeat. "Well, while you two discuss Presten Campbell and *Dead on the Beach,* I'm going to go talk to Frances and Fanny, if they'll let me in the kitchen."

Jennifer didn't have to worry. The sisters not only let her in, they made her taste every concoction they had bubbling on the stove, and although they wouldn't tell her what their secret ingredients were, it wasn't difficult to distinguish the dominant flavors. Chicken stew, vegetable soup, and a succulent pot roast. But she wasn't able to convince them they were cooking too much food.

"If we end up with leftovers, we'll just package it all up and have somebody take it over to the high school," Fanny said, sprinkling something bright green into the stew pot. " 'Cause no matter what they're eating out there, is ain't gonna be better than this. Besides, the market was most generous with their donations, and we got us enough food to feed an army. And if we don't cook it up, it's just gonna go to waste." She looked toward the door. "What did ya do with Emma Morrison? Tie her up to a post? That woman has been drivin' us crazy!"

"Well, she hasn't been driving me crazy," Frances said. "I've been too busy with my cooking to give her a second thought." She reached in her apron pocket. "You two turn your backs now. I've got some ingredients that have to go into the soup. That's it, all the way around."

Fanny made a face. "You'd think her veggie soup is the only soup in the world. Well, you just ask her about the time she put in too much pepper. I had a sneezing fit that lasted days. Had to dump in a whole loaf of bread to soak up the mess, and we still had to eat it one-half teaspoon at a time, with ten minutes in between. I remember one time . . ." Fanny's words trailed off, and she scowled. "What on earth is that?"

Fanny was talking about the deep, fervent wails that were coming from the social hall, and Jennifer couldn't imagine. But whoever it was, it sounded like their heart was breaking.

Thinking it might be Patty, Jennifer hurried out of the kitchen. But it wasn't Patty. It was Janna Kircher, the jewelers' daughter, whose pretty face was awash with tears. Her father had collapsed and was in the hospital, and wasn't expected to make it through the night. Wes had heard her sobs, and rushed in to comfort her, but Janna was beyond solace. And her words were full of anguish. "It's the flood and that terrible robbery. Daddy lost everything, Pastor Gray, and his heart just wasn't strong enough. Mama is with him at the hospital, and I know I should be, too, but I thought if I came here . . . if I could spend some time in church. . . ."

Wes put a comforting arm around her shoulder. "Come along, Janna. We'll go to the church together, and have a nice long talk with God."

"Oh my, that's so sad!" Millie said after they left the room. "Here today, gone tomorrow, which just proves how important it is to live each day to the fullest, and make peace with those we love. *Now* do you understand, Patty?"

Jennifer had no idea what Millie was talking about, but apparently Patty did, because she was weeping again. But then there wasn't a dry eye in the room, and that included Fred, who looked ghastly. Wondering if he really was ill, Jennifer picked up Peaches, and placed a cheek against her head. Nothing seemed that important now. Not the flood, or even the lost homes. Nothing was more important than being alive.

Emma cleared her throat. "I think we should all say a prayer for that poor family. It's truly heartbreaking."

"Amen," Frances said. "We heard, and we think it's just the saddest thing."

"That we do," Fanny said, wiping at her eyes. "Why, I remember when Janna Kircher was knee high, riding her bike all over town with her blond pigtails a-flyin' in the breeze. And I remember when her daddy opened that jewelry store. Took every cent he had, but he was so proud." She reached for Peaches, and hugged her close. "Well, we ain't gonna do one speck of good standing around with long faces. Frances and me, well, we don't go to church much, but that don't mean we don't believe in God. And like our daddy always used to say, God don't care if you're a-sittin' in church or in your livin' room. He'll hear you. So we can all pray for that man in our own way.

"Now, we've got us some mighty fine vittles ready and waitin' in the kitchen, and there ain't nothin' that makes a body feel better than proper nourishment. Then we're gonna have a sing-along for that man and his family, and while we're at it, we can thank God for lettin' us get this far along in life."

Ken blew his nose. "You ladies need some help in the kitchen?"

Fanny peered at Ken over the top of her granny glasses. "Guess we could use some help, long as you don't take any pictures."

Ken smiled. "I wouldn't dream of it, Fanny, at least not without your permission."

"Hmm. Well, maybe later, after we get home. Guess I wouldn't mind havin' a picture with little Peaches wearing one of her pretty dresses."

After they left the room, Emma sighed. "You know, sometimes I find myself actually liking those crazy sisters."

Jennifer gave Emma a hug. "I know, just like sometimes I find myself actually liking that arrogant reporter."

"Hmm, well, I don't think he's so arrogant. Maybe he's a little too smug and self-assured at times, but I think that's what makes a good reporter." Emma lowered her voice. "Wonder how little Patty is taking all this? I mean, if she and her friends robbed that jewelry store, they've got to feel responsible for Ron Kircher landing in the hospital. I'd say that's why she's crying her eyes out again, but she's been doing that all day anyway. Hmm. Do you think Millie suspects the truth? You heard her when she said how important it was to make peace with your loved ones, and asked Patty if she understood. I think she meant Patty should make peace with Tom, but a body has to wonder what else the girl has told her."

"I don't think Millie would sit on something like that, Emma. It's too important."

"Unless she's trying to get the girl to fess up to it on her own. Well, the sheriff will be coming by later, so we'll see what he says." She frowned at Jennifer. "You do plan on telling the sheriff about the van, don't you?"

"Of course I'm going to tell him, Emma. He has to find out who those kids really are, for one thing, and I'm looking forward to his opinions. At the very worst, all he can do is tell us we have overactive imaginations."

Emma snorted. "Well, our overactive imaginations have helped solve many a mystery, young lady, and best we don't forget it." She sniffed the air. "I smell vegetable soup. Or is that only wishful thinking?"

"It's vegetable soup," Jennifer said, giving Emma a weary smile. "Just don't ask me what's in it."

A smile tugged at the corners of Emma's

mouth. "I might be a lot of things, but foolish isn't one of them. Hmm. Well, maybe you could answer one question? Is my church kitchen ever going to be the same?"

Chapter Six

Supper not only turned out to be uniquely different, it created appetites where there were none. Jennifer took Penelope a plate, which she'd accepted hungrily, and even the kids ate with relish, though their expressions remained glum. Fred Perkins was the only holdout, but after Millie told him that unless he snapped out of his doldrums, they were going to turn around and go home instead of going on to Omaha, he dished up a bowl of soup and forced it down. Millie was upset, too, because Fred wouldn't tell her why he'd had the clandestine meeting with

Wes, and at one point during supper, she'd accused him of acting strange in his old age. Fred had come back with, "There are a whole lot of things worse in life than old age and senility, Mama, like death and taxes." With that, he'd gone for a walk, leaving Millie to fume and fuss until he returned. And then, when he did, he wouldn't talk to her.

Now, with supper over and things a bit more relaxed, Jennifer joined Wes at a corner table where he was drinking a cup of coffee. "I love you, Grandfather," she said, kissing his cheek.

Wes smiled. "And I love you, sweetheart. What brought that on?"

"Can't I tell my favorite grandfather I love him?" She took a deep breath. "It's a lot more than that, Grandfather. When I look around at all the unhappiness, I feel so blessed to have your support and love. After Mom and Dad died, I was lucky to have you and Emma. I truly wish I had a magic wand to make all the pain go away for these people. And I'd begin with Fred Perkins. Do you have any idea what's bothering him?"

Wes took a sip of coffee, and sighed. "I

have a pretty good idea, but it's not my place to interfere. Nor can I betray Fred's confidence. About all I can do is hope and pray he makes the right decision, before Millie takes it personally, and does something foolish."

"That sounds ominous."

Wes managed a smile. "Well, I could say the same about your behavior tonight, sweetheart. Your whole demeanor has been one of impending doom."

"To be honest, it's because I've been waiting for the other shoe to drop. I wanted to talk to you earlier, but with so much going on, and then supper. . . ."

"Well, supper was certainly interesting, wasn't it?"

"Yes, it was. About as interesting as Emma and Ken's budding friendship."

Wes looked over at the twosome, who had their heads together, and grinned. "It takes one mystery lover to know one. The last I heard, they were working through the Paul Stanford mysteries, and had gotten up to *The Horseless Rider of Bayberry Street.* So, my lovely granddaughter, why all the gloom and doom?"

Jennifer gave him a brief rundown, and waited.

Finally, he said, "Boy oh boy, I don't know, sweetheart. That's pretty heavy stuff. Do you really think the kids would stick around here if they'd robbed the jewelry store? I would think they'd be long gone by now, with or without Patty Jones."

"I know, and we certainly can't accuse them of being the culprits without proof, but I have to agree with Ken. I think they stripped the van, too, so why would they do something like that if it wasn't stolen?"

"Even if they stole the van, that doesn't mean they robbed the jewelry store."

"I still have to tell the sheriff what we found, Grandfather, and what we suspect."

"Of course you do. But Jim is a good man, and he'll handle it fairly and professionally."

Millie was talking to Patty again, and Jennifer frowned. "You know, I think Millie knows what's going on, but like you and Fred Perkins, she won't betray Patty's confidence. And I think the other three know

Millie knows, and that's why they are so upset with Patty."

"Maybe, but like I said, if they were guilty of something that bad, I'm sure they would be long gone by now, with or without Patty. And now with Ron Kircher in the hospital, well, I would think knowing they are partly responsible for the man's heart attack would be devastating. That truly breaks my heart. Poor Evie. She must be frantic."

"Maybe we should call the hospital."

"Janna promised to call with an update."

"Is she going to be okay?"

"I think so. She's young and strong, and she has her mama. They'll be able to draw strength from each other. On a more pleasant note, do you think the sisters would give Emma the recipes for that good chicken stew and pot roast?"

Jennifer looked over at the sisters, who were sitting at a table, playing with the chimp, and smiled. "Fanny fixed the pot roast, so she might, but to tell you the truth, I don't think Frances would give her recipe to Julia Child for a million dollars. You know, they've really been wonderful through this whole thing. Emma said she's going to ask a few of her friends at the senior citizens' center to help patch up the sisters' roof."

"Oh, she did, did she? Next, she'll be inviting them to the house for supper, and getting them involved with the campaign. Speaking of the campaign, have you heard from Willy?"

"I've talked to him a couple of times on the phone. Right about now, the mayoral race is the last thing on his mind. And on that note, have you heard about Mayor Attwater?"

Wes grinned. "I heard. I also heard old man Fenten is going to sue his pants off. Fenten wasn't injured in the collision, but the frosty machine is toast. Ah, here comes the sheriff. Maybe you should take him into my office to have your little talk. Or maybe you should take him to the house, where you can give him a good cup of coffee. This stuff is beginning to taste like a two-dollar can of varnish."

Jennifer nodded, but she was watching the two stranded young couples. All four of them looked so tense and jittery at the sight of the sheriff, she expected them to bolt for the door.

The sheriff went to the center of the room, and clapped his hands for attention. "It's been a long day, so if I can have everybody's attention for a minute, I have a few announcements to make before I get to the socializing and can relax with a cup of coffee." He looked around. "Where's Penelope?"

"In the Sunday-school room with her cats," Emma said.

"Want me to get her?" Ken asked.

"Uh-huh, because some of this has to do with her."

"I'm here," Penelope said wearily. "I saw you pull up, sheriff, and I pray the news is good."

"It is. The levees are holding, and the water is receding. We also have a favorable weather forecast, so it looks like the worst is over. You'll be able to go home in the morning, Penelope."

Penelope let out an audible sigh. "Thank goodness!"

"Uh-huh, well, I think a whole bunch of us have had guardian angels sitting on our shoulders." He looked at Fred and Millie Perkins. "The garage will be delivering your car about noon tomorrow, and that's just about the time they'll be opening the highway. Wish it could be sooner, but tomorrow is better than next week." He nodded at the kids. "Sorry to say your van is still sitting out in the mud, but I've got old Grundy's solemn word he'll get to it first thing tomorrow afternoon."

Grumbles followed, and Patty lowered her eyes.

"Okay, now for the best news yet. Janna Kircher told me she stopped by, so you know all about what happened to her daddy. Well, I'm happy to say he's gonna pull through. They had to do a bypass, but he came through it just fine. Come to find out, having that heart attack was a blessing in disguise. If he hadn't had the surgery when he did, he could've had a major heart attack that would have taken him just like that." He snapped his fingers. "Didn't get a chance to talk to him because he was still in intensive care, but his wife can pass on the good news.

Except for one piece, we've recovered the stolen jewelry."

Gasps went up, and the sheriff grinned. "I know. I have a hard time believing it myself. Nettie Balkin found the package sitting on a desk in the storage room this afternoon. For those of you who aren't familiar with our office, we have a storage room in the rear. The door opens onto an alley, and Nettie had the door open for ventilation. She claims with all the rain, the office was starting to smell like dirty socks. She told me she heard a noise in the storage room earlier, but we've got us a big old yellow tomcat that prowls around and comes in whenever the door is open, so she didn't give it a second thought."

Jennifer whispered to Wes, "Did anybody leave the social hall this afternoon?"

"Uh-huh. The two young fellows went for a walk about four o'clock."

"Were they gone long enough to walk the five blocks to the sheriff's office?"

"They were. I'd say they were gone a good hour."

"So," the sheriff went on, "it looks like our robber, or looter, had a change of heart."

Peaches waddled over to the sheriff, and he picked her up. "Well, little lady, what do you think about that? I'd say the crook wasn't really a crook after all. Just some poor misguided soul who was met with a serious temptation when he found the jewelry store door open, and he made the wrong decision."

Peaches pulled her lips back from her teeth, and let out a series of whoops and chortles.

"Boy oh boy," Wes said, looking around the room. "That's what I like to see. Smiling faces."

The sheriff put Peaches down, and took her hand. "Now, I'll have that cup of coffee."

"Sheriff . . ."

The sheriff turned. Patty was on her feet, wringing her hands.

"Don't do it," Tom Davis grumbled. "You're gonna regret it."

Jane Brown piped up, "It's *her* life, and her call all the way, Tom, so butt out."

Patty shot Tom a look of pure exasperation, and said, "I'd like to talk to you, Sheriff. It's important."

The sheriff nodded. "Okay, the coffee can wait. Go on, Peaches. Be a good girl, and go over to Frances and Fanny." He smiled at Patty. "You want to talk here? Or in private?"

"I-in private."

"You can use my office," Wes said. "Nobody will bother you, and you'll be comfortable."

"Lordy, what do you make of that?" Emma said, joining Jennifer and Wes at the table.

Ken pulled up a chair, too, and said, "Sounds like she's going to confess to the sheriff, but I don't understand why. If they returned the jewelry, they are home free, because nobody can prove anything."

"Maybe she wants to tell him about the stolen van," Emma reasoned.

Wes shook his head. "No way. You think those two disgruntled young men would allow her to confess something like that? If she goes down, they all go down."

Perplexed, Jennifer said, "What then?"

Millie, who was standing close by, dropped to a chair. "I hope you don't think I was eavesdropping, but I know what's going on. They didn't rob the jewelry store, and they didn't steal the van. Well, not exactly."

Emma scowled. "Not exactly?"

"Oh, my. Little Patty swore me to secrecy, but if she's telling the sheriff. . . . Well, you'll probably find out about it from the sheriff anyway, and I truly don't want you to think badly of her, or her friends . . ." Millie gave a big sigh. "Patty is a runaway. She and her daddy had a falling out, and she took her daddy's van. Her friends were planning a trip across country, but couldn't afford to buy a vehicle. So Patty had the transportation, and they made the plans."

Jennifer said, "Then Patty is underage?"

"She's seventeen. The other three are in their early twenties."

Wes shook his head. "I take it they aren't from Council Bluffs."

"No, they aren't. Patty didn't say where they are from, but I'm sure she'll tell the sheriff. When the storm hit, and the van got stuck in the mud, they had to make some quick decisions. Bob, Jane, and Tom were all for hitchhiking to California, but Patty wanted to call her daddy. She regretted the whole thing, and wanted to go home. But because she was underage, and the van belonged to Patty's father, Bob was afraid they'd get in serious trouble. So, they stripped the van and were headed for the next town, when the sheriff picked them up. When they found out the road was closed, they knew they were stuck, and had to bluff their way through."

"And their last names? Ken asked. "I have the feeling they aren't Smith, Brown, Davis, and Jones."

"No, they aren't, but she didn't tell me what they were. The only reason she confided in me was because she had to talk to somebody, and she said I had a kind, understanding face." She sighed, and looked at her husband, who was off in a corner, sulking. "Now all I have to do is get my husband to confide in me. I know something has him terribly upset, but he won't tell me what it is. Anyway, I told Patty she should call her father, because life is too short to be adrift from your loved ones."

"What about her mama?" Emma asked.

"Her mama died when she was little. No brothers or sisters."

"Lordy, her papa must be frantic!" Emma said.

"That's what I told her. I had no idea she was going to tell the sheriff, and to tell you the truth, I don't know why she is. Unless she thinks he has a trusting face, too, and can help her, like maybe be the go-between with her father. And I'll tell you something else. I thought those three would be long gone the minute Patty said she wanted to talk to the sheriff, but they're still here, so that tells me they are going to stand by her, no matter what, as well as face the consequences."

There was more to the conversation, but Jennifer wasn't listening. The kids had been exonerated, so if they hadn't robbed the jewelry store, who had? Wondering if it even mattered now, now that the jewelry had been returned, Jennifer excused herself, and went over to sit with the sisters, who were trying to teach the chimp to play peekaboo.

"We know she's supposed to be a slow learner," Frances said, tweaking Peaches under the chin, "but we think she didn't have the right teacher, that's all. You look sad, Jennifer. Should be a time for smiling."

Fanny bobbed her head. "Should be a time for smilin', not frownin'. Should've brought along some of our elixir. It's good for all sorts of things, ya know, like warts and ingrown toenails, tummy aches and headaches, and even a bad case of the blahs."

"I know I should be smiling," Jennifer said. "We have so much to be thankful for. And I'd like to thank you for all you've done to help out. You have your own problems, yet you've never once mentioned your little cottage, and what you might find when you get home."

Frances shook her head. "That little cottage will be standing long after we're gone, so there is no point in worrying about it. So we might have a little plaster on the kitchen floor, or a storm-blown air vent in the ceiling, but it won't be the first time. Probably won't be the last. I think about all we have to worry about is getting down that old mud-hollow road. Guess we'll be doing that tomorrow. Going home, like everybody else."

"Emma plans to call on a few of her senior citizen friends with carpenter skills to help repair your roof," Jennifer said. "She says it's the least she can do after all your help."

Fanny beamed. "You hear that, sister? It'll be a good time to have a little party. A roof-fixin' party, and Emma Morrison can be the guest of honor."

The thought of it finally brought a smile to Jennifer's face.

Fanny poked her sister on the arm. "You see that, Sister? Little Jennifer Gray is smilin'. Now if we can get those young folks and Fred Perkins a-smilin', we'll have a little party right here, to celebrate."

Frances said, "Well, we sure don't have to put a smile on the sheriff's face. Here he comes with that young girl, and he's grinning from ear to ear."

The sheriff spoke to Wes, and then to the kids, and although Jennifer couldn't hear all of it, she caught the most important part. Patty had called her father. They had their differences to work out, but he'd been forgiving and loving, and was coming to pick the kids up the next day. The sheriff had also made arrangements for the kids to stay at the hotel on their last night in Calico, and planned to drive them over as soon as they could get their things together. A few weepy moments followed, while Patty and Millie hugged and said their good-byes, but it was a good feeling to have a happy ending, when only an hour ago it hadn't seemed possible.

"Well, now," Fanny said after they'd gone. "I think we should get out the apple juice, Sister, and maybe some of that apple cobbler you've got a-hidin' in the cupboard. I know you made it for Pastor Wes, but at a time like this, when we're all gonna have to say good-bye, I think he'd be happy to share. What do you think, Jennifer?"

Jennifer got up and kissed their leathery cheeks. "I think Grandfather would be delighted to share the apple cobbler, but don't be surprised if he asks you for the recipe. He's grown quite fond of your cooking."

Frances touched her cheek where Jennifer kissed her, and flushed. "Hmm. Well, I don't know about Fanny, but I wouldn't mind giving Pastor Wes a few of my recipes."

"Wouldn't mind, either," Fanny said, wiping at a tear that had slipped down her cheek. “Hmm. Well, looks like I got somethin’ in my eye. Can’t have that, while I’m tryin’ to pour the apple juice. Come along, Sister. Best we be gettin’ to our duties, and that includes shining up the kitchen for Emma Morrison.”

Frances rolled her eyes, and gave Jennifer a helpless shrug. “Times can change, things can change, even feelings can change, but nobody is going to change that bossy sister of mine.” She started to walk away, and then turned and faced Jennifer. “I want to thank you, young lady.”

“For what?” Jennifer asked.

“For that kiss, and just for being you, Jennifer Gray. You’ve been a good friend, and that’s something this old body will never forget.”

Jennifer held Peaches while Frances strode off toward the kitchen, and blinked back a few tears of her own.

Chapter Seven

If it wasn't for the farmland that had been flooded northwest of town, someone passing through Calico would have seen a community simply cleaning up after a major storm, unaware of the effort it had taken to save homes and lives, or how close they had come to having the entire town flooded. Or how many lives had been changed as a result, like the Cutlers, who had lost everything, and Ron Kircher, who would have to alter his lifestyle because of his heart. Some of the changes had been less dramatic, but meaningful nonetheless, like the stately elm tree at the corner of Lincoln and Park Streets that had toppled at the height of the storm. It had been a landmark, going back to when Calico hadn't been much more than a dusty settlement, and now it was gone. A creek now ran through Calico Park, cutting a path through the kiddie playground, picnic area, and rose gardens. And the jogging trails along the greenbelt had simply crumbled away into the river.

The river had changed, too, as the high, swiftly moving water had cut off large chunks of the shoreline and had ripped away the small marina downstream, taking the smaller boats with it. And Route 5 had changed, too. Deadman's Curve had become narrower and more treacherous, and fencing was down for miles, allowing cattle to roam freely. The crop loss was significant, even for the farmers who hadn't been flooded out, which all translated into hard economic times ahead. Recovery wouldn't be easy, and Jennifer was quite sure the heartbreaking stories would continue to emerge, slowly but profoundly. It was also a time for dependable leadership because so many weighty decisions would have to be made, and the timing couldn't have been worse, because the mayoral election was still four months away, and Mayor Attwater was a man filled with apathy. If a problem crossed his desk, he would wave a hand and say, "You fix it." And so the town council would be left to make the decisions and "fix it," and every one of them seemed to be at least eighty years old, and living in the dark ages. And, at the moment, the mayor seemed to be more concerned with his dispute with old man Fenten than the plight of the town. Jennifer became angry when she read the morning paper. There were bold headlines all about the mayor's auto accident, and pages of nonsensical drivel, but she hadn't been able to find one mention of Ron Kircher's heart attack. And the only mention of the storm had been on page three, touting Elmer Dodd as the town hero, because he was working around the clock to assure the citizens that Calico would rise above its difficulties, and prosper. Working around the clock giving out vote-getting smiles and blowing smoke was more to the point, and Jennifer had promptly used the paper to line the carrying cases and cages to transport Penelope Davis's cats home, which had been an event in itself. It had taken an hour to get Penelope and her babies home and settled, and even though Ben kept saying he had to get to the clinic, Penelope had insisted they stay for a cup of coffee. Jennifer understood. It was as though the camaraderie they had all shared at the church had come to an end, and she didn't want to say good-bye.

It had been the same for the Cromwell sisters, too, whose colorful morning antics had only been a delay. With all the hardships and inconveniences, they had enjoyed their stay at the church. Emma had finally swooshed them out, after making them promise if their little cottage was uninhabitable, they would come back to the church without an argument. They promised, and seemed delighted they'd been given the invitation.

Now, driving her Jeep Cherokee along the streets she loved, on her way back to the church, Jennifer waved at familiar faces and felt the warmth of the sun, and their smiles, all the way to her heart. Stores were reopening, even on the streets that had been flooded. Though there was still a thick layer of gooey mud, people wore boots and plodded along, trying to make the best of it.

It was early, barely eleven o'clock, and although Jennifer planned to spend the afternoon at the clinic, Ben wasn't expecting her until after the Perkinses' car was delivered, and they were on their way to Omaha. And that wouldn't be until noon. So because she had a little time on her hands, she decided to stop by Willy Ashton's office, on the off chance he might be there. When she'd talked to him on the phone the night before, he wasn't sure how the day would go. The court system had virtually stopped because of the flood, and even Judge Stoker and Judge Thurman had been out sandbagging. And now there was the cleanup, and no matter where you looked, somebody needed help. Willy said his office was also in total disarray, so he felt betwixt and between.

Willy's office was in the only professional building in town, and faced the courthouse.

It was convenient for Willy, because he spent so much time in court, but Jennifer supposed all that would change once he was elected mayor. There would still be some cases he could handle, provided there weren't any conflicts of interest, but he also had a lot of plans for the town, which would definitely take his undivided attention. "But," as he kept saying, "I'm not in the mayor's office yet, so the best thing to do is just take each day as it comes along, and hope for the best." Jennifer had all the confidence in the world that Willy was going to be elected mayor, and simply wouldn't listen to that kind of talk.

Willy's door was open, and Jennifer found him chin deep in folders. His blue eyes twinkled at the corners when he saw her, and he ran a hand through his tousled dark hair.

"Well, this is a surprise," he said, giving her a hug.

"Surprised me, too," Jennifer said, looking around at the clutter. "You need a secretary."

"Can't afford a secretary, and where

would I put one? I can't even find the room for another file cabinet."

Willy was wearing jeans, boots, and a rumpled blue shirt, and his eyes were red-rimmed. She gave him a level look, and said, "You haven't been to bed, have you?"

Willy shrugged. "I can catch up on my sleep later. Right now, this seems paramount, and then this afternoon, I'm pitching in to help the Fentens clean up the mess. They've managed to get the front of the store boarded up, but the inside is still in a muddle."

"Did you read the morning paper?" Jennifer asked, sitting down in a chair near his desk.

"I did, and found it a bit much."

"Uh-huh, well, I used the paper to line the carrying cases and cages to transport Penelope's cats. That's how much I thought of it."

"I take it you got Penelope and the cats home safe and sound?"

"Yes, and the Cromwell sisters finally left, so that only leaves Millie and Fred Perkins. The garage is delivering their car around noon, and I'd like to be there to say good-bye."

Willy tossed a folder on the desk. "You brought me up-to-date when we talked on the phone last night, Jenny, but it's what you didn't say that made me wonder what's really going on. Care to share?"

"I told you everything, Willy."

"Sure, you gave me all the particulars, but I could tell something was bothering you, and whatever it was is *still* bothering you."

At that moment, Jennifer finally realized why she'd stopped by Willy's office. She'd wanted to see him and touch base, but it was more than that. And it was important. She felt her cheeks flush, and lowered her eyes. "Ken Hering wants me to go out with him, Willy. . . ."

"Like in going out on a date?" Willy asked, raising a brow.

"Yeah, like that. I guess I just wanted to know how you feel about it."

"More important, how do *you* feel about it?"

"To tell you the truth, I don't know. A few days ago I detested the man, and now . . .

Well, he isn't the arrogant jerk I thought he was, for one thing, and he's been a lot of help. He even stood up for you when Elmer and Collin stopped by the church."

"How did *I* get into it?" Willy asked.

"Norman Fuller made some derogatory remarks, and Ken told him he was out of line, that you weren't there to defend yourself, so Fuller had no right to insult you, or words to that effect. Charlie Waters reminded Ken he worked for *The Calico Review*, and because *The Calico Review* is backing Elmer, he all but implied that by sticking up for you, Ken was being subversive. And then Jack Boodie jumped all over Charlie Waters, and the sheriff had to break it up."

Willy shook his head. "Sounds like I missed a good party. So, because you've decided Ken Hering isn't a creep, and came to my defense, you want to go out with him. Maybe I'm missing something else here, Jenny. I thought our relationship was based on trust and friendship. So why did you think it was necessary to ask for my permission? That is what you're asking, isn't it?"

Jennifer sighed. "Maybe I was hoping you'd tell me what I should do. Ken said he didn't want to step on your toes, and was quite honest about his feelings. And I was honest with him. I told him you and I are good friends, but we aren't really romantically involved. At least not now . . . Not seriously. I don't know, Willy. I haven't dated anybody but you since coming home from vet school, and maybe that's been a mistake. Maybe this whole conversation is a mistake. I didn't want to upset you, yet I can see you're disturbed. I can see it in your eyes, and the way you're holding your mouth."

Willy got up and walked to the window. And it was a long moment before he said, "You know how much I care about you, Jenny. And maybe that's the biggest part of the problem. We know each other too well, and we've been taking each other for granted. We've had a comfortable, uncomplicated relationship, and maybe it's time we faced a few facts. First of all, if I win the election, my life is going to be one big roller-coaster ride, twenty-four hours a day, because there is no way I'm going to sit in the mayor's office and twiddle my thumbs. . . ." He sighed. "This isn't coming out right, Jenny. I'll always have time for you and the closeness we share, but I'd be foolish if I expected you to sit around twiddling *your* thumbs, waiting for me to block out a few free minutes on my calendar. Well, nuts. That doesn't sound right, either."

"I know what you're trying to say, Willy. Just because I might date Ken Hering, or even somebody else along the line, it won't change our friendship. And that works both ways. If you want to date somebody else, I'll understand."

Willy smiled. "Then I don't see a problem, unless we make it one." He winked at her. "Still friends?"

"Still friends," she said, feeling a tightness in her throat. It had suddenly occurred to her that maybe she'd wanted him to react differently. Maybe even throw a temper tantrum, react jealously, but above all, proclaim his love for her, and demand she forget all about Ken Hering. And it was so foolish. She loved Willy, but she wasn't *in* love with him, and she knew that was the way he felt about her. So what then?

Willy was studying her intently, and finally said, "I see some apprehension, Jenny. Are you frightened at the thought of dating Ken Hering?"

She took a deep breath. "Maybe. I don't want to get romantically involved with anyone, Willy. I like my life just the way it is."

"Then I can't advise you on what to do. This one comes from the heart, *your* heart, therefore the decision has to be yours. But if you want my opinion, you shouldn't be making such a big deal out of it. Dating the man doesn't mean you have to make a lifetime commitment. But you'd better be forewarned. If he gives you any problems, he'll have to deal with me."

"I'll remember that," she said, giving him a hug, feeling as though she were saying good-bye to an important part of her life. "Call me?"

Willy smiled. "You can count on it."

Jennifer hurried out, before Willy could see the tears in her eyes.

* * *

It was almost noon when Jennifer walked into the social hall, and found herself in the middle of another upheaval. For some strange reason, Fred Perkins wanted to stay in Calico a few more days, and had taken it upon himself to rent a room at the hotel. Millie couldn't understand his reasoning, and had spent the morning arguing with the stubborn man. And if that wasn't bad enough, Tootsie Marie, who had been sick the night before, was worse. She was vomiting again, and demonstrating a great deal of stress and discomfort.

Though Fred was concerned, he also used the dog's illness to his advantage, claiming, "Good thing we weren't on the road when this happened, Mama. You know what it's like to travel with a sick dog?"

Millie's reply to that had been, "I know exactly what it's like. I'm the one who always ends up cleaning the carrying case, just like I cleaned it up a few minutes ago, and a few before that, and twice during the night, and quite frankly, Papa, I'm ready to wash my hands of the whole thing. In case you've forgotten, our son is waiting for us in Omaha.

Well, *you* can call him this time, and tell him why we've been delayed."

Wes and Emma had stayed out of it, but Jennifer could see the concern on their faces, and she knew what they were thinking. The Perkinses had arrived at the church under difficult circumstances at best, and yet they had remained happy and cheerful, even when everybody around them had been full of gloom and doom. And now, just a few days later, the smiles were not only gone, but the couple were at each other's throats. It was as though some black cloud had come along and settled over them, filling them with anger and misery.

Jennifer quickly examined Tootsie Marie, wondering if Millie and Fred's angry words might be the reason for her upset stomach, but just as quickly, she realized it was something much more serious. For one thing, the little dog's pulse was erratic, and her temperature was subnormal.

"I'm afraid I'm going to have to take her to the clinic," Jennifer said, holding Tootsie Marie close. "I can't make a diagnosis here, but I'd say she's quite ill."

Millie's eyes filled with tears. "Oh, no! Then it isn't just a tummy upset? I was sure that was all it was. She's had them before during stressful situations, and this whole thing has been so hard on her."

"It's been hard on all of us," Fred muttered glumly. He scratched Tootsie Marie's head. "Well, do what you have to do, Jennifer. Mama and I aren't going anywhere, except to the hotel, and we won't do that until we hear from you."

Jennifer wasted no time getting on the road, and the drive didn't take long, but even so, Tootsie Marie seemed worse by the time she finally pulled into the parking area behind the clinic.

"What's this?" Ben asked, meeting Jennifer at the door.

"It's Tootsie Marie, but I haven't a clue as to what's wrong with her," Jennifer said, heading for the emergency examining room. "She's been vomiting since last night, but this is more than a stomach upset, Ben. Take a look for yourself."

Ben placed Tootsie Marie on the table, examined her quickly, and then shook his head. "I'd say she has some sort of a bowel obstruction. You'd better call the Perkinses while I get the X rays, and you'd better prepare them for the inevitable. We're going to have to operate, Jennifer, and the sooner the better."

An hour and a half later, with Tootsie Marie resting comfortably in the recovery room, Jennifer and Ben went out to the little patio area behind the clinic to take a well-deserved break and discuss their dilemma. It was more of a dilemma than ever now, after Jennifer had placed the after-surgery call to Millie Perkins. Jennifer had gotten the expected tears of relief because the surgery had been a complete success, but when she told Millie they'd found a diamond and gold brooch in the little dog's intestines, she hadn't expected Millie to say, "Well, my goodness, where do you suppose she got a hold of that?"

"Then it isn't yours?" Jennifer had asked incredulously.

"No, it isn't. You say the pin was stuck in her belly?"

"In her intestines," Jennifer replied.

"There was some internal bleeding, and we had to remove a small section of intestine, but she'll never miss it. You can also be thankful you weren't on the road when this happened. I'll be bringing her to the church in a few hours. Normally I'd keep her here overnight, but I think she'll recuperate much faster if she can see you, and of course I'll be there to keep an eye on her."

"Then should we plan to stay at the church instead of going to the hotel?" Millie asked, almost hopefully.

"It would be best, Millie. But I don't think you'll have to stay in the social hall. I'm sure Emma and my grandfather will agree you'll be much more comfortable in our guest room at the house. I think we've all seen enough of the social hall."

Millie's reply had been firm and concise. "I'm grateful for your generosity, but I can't speak for Fred. Well, if he still wants to go to the hotel after this, he can just go!"

"So, what do you make of it?" Ben said, looking at the brooch resting on the picnic table between them.

Jennifer took a sip of coffee, and sighed. "You don't want to know what I think, Ben."

"Uh-huh, then it's probably what I'm thinking. Tootsie Marie's carrying case is a standard airline issue, and can be purchased all across the U.S. of A. We've got three of them ourselves. They come in three sizes. Small, medium, and large, but they are all made the same way. The inside floor is protected by a sheet of removable fiberboard, notched with tiny holes to allow for drainage, should the animal have an accident. Below the fiberboard, there is a two-inch-high space, the length and width of the case. Plenty of room to conceal a handful of baubles, like diamond rings, gold chains, earrings, and a diamond and gold brooch."

Jennifer felt her heart twist. "But why? Why would Fred Perkins do something like that?"

"Who says it was Fred? Maybe it was Millie. Or maybe they were in on it together. It all fits when you think about it. You say their dispositions, as well as their marriage, has deteriorated over the last couple of days. They're arguing all the time, and their smiles are gone. We also know the crook, or crooks, returned the valuables. Probably had a change of heart, but maybe returning the stuff wasn't enough. If it's Fred, or Millie, or both, they know they are partly responsible for putting Ron Kircher in the hospital. That spells out stress and a lot of guilty feelings in my book, and that could explain why they are on edge. Might even explain why Fred isn't in any hurry to leave for Omaha yet. Maybe he wants to be sure Ron is going to make it, no matter what favorable reports have been released by the hospital. You know, wait until the man is out of intensive care, and is walking up and down the hospital corridors."

Jennifer lifted her face to the warm afternoon sun, but still felt chilled. "Unfortunately, I have to agree with you. Everything fits. And Fred certainly had the opportunity all those times he was out walking Tootsie Marie. And it's very likely when he gathered up the jewelry to turn it in, he inadvertently left a piece behind, a piece that was overlooked again when Millie cleaned the case. But Tootsie Marie found it, and even that makes sense. We both know the fiberboard has to be dried out before it can be replaced in the case. During that time, they would've put Tootsie Marie in the case without the protective covering. So she found the 'overlooked' brooch, and swallowed it. But I have to wonder about the time frame, Ben." Jennifer rubbed a hand across her eyes. "The Perkinses arrived at the church the day we rescued Bosworth off the Cutlers' roof. That was also the day the Kirchers had to evacuate the store. In the confusion, they left the door open. And that was the day of the robbery. But Fred didn't take Tootsie Marie on any walks that day. It was raining buckets, and he took her out to the overhang in front of the social hall. Nor was he acting strange. It wasn't until the next day that he had a major case of the grumpies. And there is something else I haven't mentioned. Yesterday, Grandfather had a secretive talk with Fred in his office. Last night, Grandfather told me he knew what's bothering the man, why he's been acting like a toad, but he couldn't tell me because he didn't want to betray the man's trust. Well, trust goes just so far, and if Fred confided in him about the robbery, I simply can't believe Grandfather would keep quiet about it."

Ben scratched his chin. "I agree, but the fact remains, Tootsie Marie swallowed that brooch, and if it doesn't belong to Millie, who does it belong to? For sure, I don't think we should start making accusations until we have a few more answers. Like maybe the brooch belongs to one of the other ladies who were staying in the social hall."

Jennifer shook her head. "I can't think of a time when Tootsie Marie was out of the carrying case, other than those few times Fred took her for a walk."

"So maybe Tootsie Marie found the brooch out on the road somewhere, and gobbled it up when Fred wasn't looking," Ben reasoned. "It's pretty small. Wouldn't be hard to overlook."

Jennifer picked up the brooch, and turned it over in her hand. "I know a way we can get the answer, Ben. At least a way to find out if this belongs to the Kirchers."

Ben sighed. "You're going to take it to the hospital and ask them. I guess it's the only way. If it doesn't belong to them, we can relax, and concentrate on finding the rightful owner."

It sounded so simple, but it wasn't, because deep down, Jennifer knew the brooch had been taken in the robbery, and the next step would be to go to the sheriff. And it broke her heart.

Chapter Eight

It was a little before five when Jennifer walked into the sheriff's office, and placed the brooch on his desk. "I thought you might want to see this," she said, dropping into the nearest chair. "I was afraid I wouldn't get here in time. I know you like to close up around five."

The sheriff returned, "Under normal circumstances, but things have hardly been normal. The last two nights, I haven't gotten out of here until after ten. And boy, has Ida been complaining." He picked up the brooch, and turned it over in his hand. "This looks familiar."

Jennifer took a deep breath. "Only because you have a description of it on file. When Evie Kircher took inventory of the jewelry you recovered, she said one piece was missing, right?"

"Whoa. A tiny diamond and gold brooch in the shape of a butterfly. I'm going to have to ask you where you found it, but I have the feeling I'm not gonna like the answer."

Jennifer gave him a detailed accounting, along with her suspicions, and watched his face reflect a dozen different emotions before he said, "The dog could have picked up the brooch anywhere, and even if it was in the carrying case, how are we gonna prove it? Or that Fred Perkins put it there? Or more important, do we want to?" He shook his head wearily. "I don't know, Jennifer. I've been sworn to uphold the law, so where in blue blazes does something like this fit in? If Fred and Millie Perkins are the culprits, there has to be a good reason, because I don't believe for one minute they are crooks. And like you said, what about the time frame?

They were both at the church the day of the robbery, so who can figure? Did you tell the Kirchers about your suspicions?"

"No, I didn't. Ron Kircher was asleep when I got to the hospital, so I talked to Evie, but didn't go into details, other than to say I wanted to make sure the brooch belonged to them before I turned it over to you." Jennifer looked at Nettie's empty desk. "Did Nettie go home?"

"Yeah, she did, and I've given her the next couple of days off. Her basement is full of mud and goo, and she says the whole house smells like a swamp. She's hired Jasper Willis's two strapping sons to clean it up. Lots of work out there for those who want it, and lots of money being spent. We're headed for hard times, Jennifer. Yet I keep telling myself it could've been worse. A tornado could've whipped through, and flattened the whole town." He sighed. "You say you told Millie about the brooch when you talked to her on the phone, but she claims she doesn't know where the dog found it? Well, maybe she *doesn't* know. Maybe Fred is the culprit, and that's why he's been acting so strange.

Guilt can do a lot to a person, like twisting you up inside. If he's our thief, he must've had a fit when he found out you were gonna have to put Tootsie Marie under the knife. If it hadn't been for that, they'd be halfway to Omaha by now."

"That's something else, Ben. Before they found out about Tootsie Marie, Fred announced they were going to stay in town a few more days. He even rented a room at the hotel. Millie was the one who had the fit. She reminded him that their son was waiting for them in Omaha, and this time, *he* could make the call and explain why they were going to be delayed. That doesn't sound like a man who is in a hurry to get away."

"Sounds to me like a man who doesn't want to go to Omaha. Like I said, who can figure."

Jennifer bit at her bottom lip. "Grandfather might have some of the answers, Sheriff Cody. He had a long, private talk with Fred last night, and then later, he all but told me he knew what was bothering Fred, but he couldn't discuss it because he didn't want to betray the man's confidence."

The sheriff's eyes narrowed in thought. "Wes is a good man, and as honest as they come, but I can't see him protecting a crook, unless he has a darned good reason."

"Nor can I," Jennifer said wearily. "Grandfather did say one thing, though. It didn't make any sense to me then, and it still doesn't, but I have the feeling it's important. When I asked him if he knew what was troubling Fred, he said he had a pretty good idea, and although he couldn't talk about it, he hoped and prayed that Fred made the right decision, before Millie took it personally, and did something foolish. What do you make of that?"

"I don't know, Jennifer. It doesn't make any sense to me, either." He looked at the clock on the wall. "Are you heading home now?"

"Yes, and I'm dreading it."

"Well, I'd go with you, but I have some errands to run first. It might be a couple of hours, but I'll stop by on my way home."

"And then?"

The sheriff shrugged. "And then, I think we'd better pray for a miracle."

* * *

Bracing herself, and wearing her brightest smile, Jennifer walked into the cheery kitchen where Wes and Emma were preparing supper, and gave hugs around, before she said, "Where are the Perkinses?"

Emma heaved a giant sigh. "We thought the best place to keep Tootsie Marie would be in your granddaddy's study, where the poor little thing can be cozy and warm by the fireplace. So that's where she is, and the last time I looked in, Millie was cuddling her doggie, and crying her eyes out."

"Oh, no, is Tootsie Marie—"

Wes broke in. "She's fine, sweetheart. It's Fred. He went into a huff, and headed for the hotel."

"And poor Millie is taking it pretty hard," Emma went on. "Fred said he likes fried chicken, so that's what we're fixing, and we spent a lot of time getting the guest room ready for their stay, along with that cozy little corner in the study for Tootsie Marie. And right in the middle of it, with no warning, Fred announced he was going to the hotel. Millie accused him of being thoughtless and inconsiderate, he accused her of being a nag, and away he went."

"When did he leave?" Jennifer asked, sitting down at the table. "Was it before or after the last time I called?"

Emma drew her brows together in thought. "I think it was after. Hmm, that's right, it was after. After Millie told us about the surgery, and how you found some sort of a pin in Tootsie Marie's tummy. We discussed that for a while, trying to figure out where she'd found it, and then Fred made his announcement."

Jennifer poured a cup of coffee from the silver carafe on the table, and lowered her eyes. "Didn't you think that was strange?"

"Of course it was strange," Emma said, "but then everything that man has been doing is strange."

Wes sighed. "With good reason."

Emma's frown deepened. "And what does that mean?"

"It means it's possible Fred robbed the jewelry store, stashed the loot in Tootsie Marie's carrying case, and when he decided to return the jewelry, he overlooked the brooch, and Tootsie Marie found it," Jennifer said. "Am I getting close, Grandfather?"

Speechless, Emma could only stare at Wes as he considered his reply. And Jennifer held her breath.

Wearily, Wes sat down at the table. "Have you talked to the sheriff?"

"Yes, and he's stopping by on his way home. I told him about your meeting with Fred, and about all those things you wouldn't tell me. I'm sorry, Grandfather, but I had to tell him."

"I know, sweetheart, and I understand. But we're talking about two different things here."

Emma angrily dredged the chicken parts in flour, sending up a cloud of white. "Lordy, what is this world coming to when we can't trust the people we know and love. You're an honest man, Wesley Gray. How could you harbor an outlaw? Oh, poor Millie. This is going to about kill her!"

"That's what Fred was worried about," Wes said. "He was afraid if Millie found out the truth, it would kill her."

Emma whirled around and harrumphed.

"Well, I can understand that. I know how I'd feel if my husband robbed a jewelry store!"

Wes shook his head. "The conversation I had with Fred had nothing to do with the jewelry store or the robbery. Fred thinks he has cancer. That's why the trip to Omaha. He's scheduled for a series of tests."

Jennifer sucked in her breath. "And Millie doesn't know about it?"

"No, she doesn't. She thought they were simply going to Omaha to visit their son. I'm not going to go into the details, except to say Fred already has himself dead and buried, and is worried sick about Millie. They don't have a lot of money, and if it is cancer, it will surely wipe them out financially. Now that I think about it, maybe he wanted to tell me so he could justify the robbery in his own mind. It also explains a lot. Like his bad mood, loss of appetite, and even why he wanted to stay on in Calico for a few more days. I think it was his way of stalling, because he didn't want to face the answers in Omaha. I also think. . . ."

Wes's words trailed off as Millie entered the kitchen. She dropped into a chair, and hugged her arms close to her body, but there were no tears in her eyes. Only understanding. "I couldn't help but overhear your conversation," she said a little raggedly. "I heard Jennifer come in, and I just wanted to say hello, and thank her for helping Tootsie Marie. . . . It's strange how one minute you think your life is over, that the man you love with all your heart no longer loves you, and then all of a sudden you find out just how much he loves you. If Fred robbed that jewelry store, he must have been desperate. But he's also a good man, and I know he must have come to his senses. That's why he decided to return the jewelry. He couldn't keep it. Not in a million years, no matter how many financial problems we have, now or in the future."

"It's also possible he's innocent," Wes reasoned. "And we can't judge him until—"

"I'm not innocent," Fred said, plodding into the kitchen. "The front door was open. . . ."

Millie quietly went into his arms, and wept. "Why didn't you tell me about the tests?" she asked finally, when she had some semblance of control.

"I didn't want to worry you. I was worried enough for the two of us, but after I talked to Wes last night, I realized I was making a mistake. He made me see what I was doing to you, and that's why I went to the hospital. That's where I've been for the last couple of hours. The tests are inconclusive, but they seem to think I have diverticulitis. That means I've got a whole bunch of little pockets sitting along my intestines, and some of them have become inflamed. It can be serious, but it can also be controlled with medication and a special diet. I thought I had stomach cancer, because that's how my dad died, and . . ." He buried his face in his wife's hair, and shuddered. "I'm so sorry, Mama. So sorry for everything."

Millie clung to him, unable to speak.

Wes cleared his throat. "Well, I think the best thing for you to do right about now is sit down and try to relax. Emma, do we have any chamomile tea? I think Millie and Fred can use a cup, and some quiet time alone."

Fred hurried on. "We have the rest of our

lives to be alone, God willing, and I have to get this off my chest, while I still have the nerve. When we got caught in that flash flood and the car was bogged down in the mud, the last thing on my mind was robbing a jewelry store. All I wanted to do was get Millie to high ground. I left her in the car because I didn't want her walking through thigh-high mud, and hiked into town for help. First couple of streets I came to had already been evacuated. And then I saw the jewelry store, with the front door wide open. I went over to close it, and then. . . ." He took a deep breath. "I've always been an honest man, so I guess a must've gone a little crazy. I saw all that jewelry inside the store, thought about Millie, and how tough it was going to be without me, and how much a few extra bucks would help out. A thousand? A couple of thousand? I had no idea what I was taking, but I knew the diamond rings and gold chains would be the most valuable. I filled my pockets, figured I'd hock the stuff in Omaha, and went out the back way. Nobody saw me. A block over, a tow truck came by, and I waved it down. The driver said it would be a while before he could get to our car, and offered to take us to the church. While Millie was getting from our car into the tow truck, I put the jewelry in Tootsie Marie's carrying case, under the fiberboard. That was also about the time I started getting a case of the jitters, and by the next morning, I knew I had to take the jewelry back. And then when that young girl came in and said her father was in the hospital . . ." Fred swallowed deeply, and couldn't go on.

Millie leaned her head against his shoulder, and closed her eyes. "You'll have to tell the sheriff," she said, barely above a whisper.

"I know, and I will the first chance I get."

"Might be sooner than you think," Wes said. "He's supposed to be stopping by here on his way home."

Fred nodded. "The sooner the better. I don't know what's going to happen to me, Mama, and it breaks my heart to think what this is going to do to you, but . . ."

"Shh," Millie said softly. "Whatever happens, we'll face it together."

Fred's plump face furrowed in pain. "And Tootsie Marie. I'm responsible for her problems, too." He looked at Jennifer with tears in his eyes. "Is she going to be okay?"

"Why don't you go see for yourself?" Jennifer said. "She's in Grandfather's study."

The relief was genuine, and he finally smiled. "Mama?"

"She's going to be just fine, Papa," Millie said, taking his arm as they left the room.

Emma wiped at her eyes. "That's so sad. Lordy, isn't there something we can do?"

Wes sighed. "About all we can do is be here for them, no matter what the outcome, and tell the sheriff how we feel. He's a compassionate man, and maybe if he understands why it happened, he might show some leniency. I'm not condoning what Fred did, you understand, but everybody can make a mistake."

Jennifer squeezed her grandfather's hand. "And you wonder why I love you."

Wes gave her a warm, impassioned smile. "I've never wondered, sweetheart. I've just been thankful, and grateful for our peaceful, rewarding life, but never once forgetting, 'there, but for the grace of God, go I.' No man is an island, and we all must learn compassion and forgiveness."

"Amen," Emma said, filling four cups with chamomile tea.

A smile played at the corners of Wes's mouth. "If we had some of the Cromwell sisters' elixir to add to the tea, it would surely brighten this dark hour."

Emma twisted her face up in a scrunch, but before she could voice her opinion, or protest, the sheriff arrived. He knocked at the back door with hesitant raps, which told Jennifer he was dreading this as much as they were.

It had taken an hour and two pots of chamomile tea for Fred to repeat his touching story to the sheriff, and although he never once tried to negate his unlawful behavior, he had touched all of their hearts in one way or another.

Finally, the sheriff ripped off several pages in his notebook, tossed them aside, and said, "How do you feel about community service, Fred? Unless this diverticulitis is going to put you under."

"I'll know more tomorrow after my appointment with the doctor, but he seemed to think I'll be just fine with the proper medication and diet, so as far as the community service . . . Well, from what I saw on the drive to the hospital, the town needs a lot of help. I'll stay as long as you want, Sheriff, and I'll do whatever you want to make this right."

"Uh-huh. Then why don't you stop by my office after you see the doctor tomorrow, and we'll go from there. You're gonna have to stick around for a few days anyway, because of your pooch, so I'd say that should about take care of it."

"I-I don't know how to thank you," Fred stammered.

"Just be happy, and look at this as a new beginning. Each and every one of us deserves a new beginning now and again.

"Now, I'd better be going. My wife is expecting me home for supper, for the first time in a week, and I'm looking forward to it." He'd reached the door before he turned and said, "For the record, I'm marking the case closed, and putting the file in the drawer with all the other unsolved mysteries. Don't have many, but every now and again one comes along that either stumps us, or just doesn't seem worth pursuing."

Jennifer walked out with the sheriff, and when they reached the patrol car, she gave him a hug. "You're the greatest, Sheriff Cody."

He flushed, and said, "And every now and again, a case comes along that makes this blamed job worth while. The Perkinses are good people, Jennifer, and nothing would be gained by making a big to-do over it."

When the car radio crackled to life, the sheriff reached through the open window and keyed the mike. "The sheriff, here."

The radio crackled again, and then, "Deputy Pressman, Sheriff Cody. We've got us a fracas out at Boodie's Roadhouse. A fender bender in the parking lot, and the two disgruntled drivers are down in the mud, slugging it out."

"Anybody we know?"

"Uh-huh. One of the Wilson brothers and

Collin Dodd. Ken Hering is here and got some pretty good pictures. Front-page stuff, if you ask me. Want me to haul 'em in?"

"No point getting the jail all muddied up. Break it up, if you have to, and then send them on their way."

The thought suddenly occurred to Jennifer out of nowhere, and before she could reason why, she said, "Can Deputy Pressman give a message to Ken Hering?"

The sheriff nodded. "Manny, is Ken Hering nearby?"

"That's a ten-four, Sheriff."

"Put him on." He handed the microphone to Jennifer. "Might as well give him the message yourself."

Jennifer took the mike, and felt her heart give a little flutter. "Ken? This is Jennifer. Emma is fixing a chicken dinner, and I thought . . . well. . . ."

Ken laughed. "If that's an invitation to dinner, pretty vet lady, the answer is yes. Just tell me where, and how soon."

"At the house, in about an hour."

"At the house in about an hour. That'll give me time to change my clothes. I'm not as muddy as Collin Dodd, but it's close. *Ciao.*"

After the sheriff got into his patrol car and keyed the mike, he winked at Jennifer. "And every now and again something comes along that proves my instincts are right on target."

"Meaning?"

"Meaning, I knew you were gonna get together with Ken Hering sooner or later."

Jennifer felt hot spots touch her cheeks. "He's only coming to dinner, Sheriff."

"Uh-huh, well, we'll see. Ida is waiting, so gotta go."

Emma was putting the chicken in the oven when Jennifer walked into the kitchen, and she was singing a little tune. She looked at Jennifer and smiled. "Decided to bake the chicken because of Fred's condition. Better for him, and healthier for us. Your granddaddy is in the dining room setting the table with the china and silver, and the Perkinses are with Tootsie Marie. They wanted to help with supper, but I thought they needed some quiet time alone. They'll be staying right here with us until Tootsie Marie can travel, and Fred has paid his debt, then they are going home. But we'll be seeing a lot of them, because Fred wants to keep the doctor at the Calico Hospital, and they'll make it a point to pass this way when they visit their son in Omaha. Now, why don't you take that bowl of fruit into the dining room. We need something for a centerpiece, and with all the flowers gone. . . ." She shook her head. "So many things are gone now, because of the storm. So many changes. . . ." She squared her shoulders. "Make sure your granddaddy is using the silver candle holders, and the tall white tapers. I want this to be a festive occasion. We all have so much to be thankful for."

"I love you," Jennifer said, kissing Emma's cheek.

"And I love you, honey, more than you'll ever know. Now scoot, before I get all weepy, and believe me, that's the last thing I want to do. I've seen enough gloomy faces and tears this past week to last a lifetime!"

"No gloomy faces or tears allowed," Wes said, padding into the kitchen. "I finished setting the table, so now what, Emma?"

Emma looked around. "Everything is under control. The vegetables are on, the potatoes are peeled, and we still have some of Fanny's apple cobbler . . ." She lowered her eyes, and a flush touched her cheeks. "though I would suppose Fanny might be bringing something else along for dessert. I haven't told Jennifer yet, Wes, but I guess now would be a good time. I called the Cromwell sisters, and invited them to join us for supper, honey. Figured they should be a part of this happy time, and join in the festivities. It's a way of thanking them for all their help, too, and of course they'll be bringing along Peaches. . . . What is it, young lady? That's a mighty sly look."

"I just invited Ken Hering to supper, too."

Wes raised a brow. "How did you manage that?"

"I talked to him over the sheriff's radio. One of the Wilson brothers and Collin Dodd got into a scuffle in the parking lot at Boodie's Roadhouse, and Ken was there taking pictures. I hope you don't mind. He likes your cooking so much, Emma, and—"

Emma clucked her tongue. "Don't mind at all. The more the merrier. Set another plate at the table, Wes, and I'd better peel a few more potatoes, but then don't suppose we'll be short in the food department, seeing as how the sisters are bringing along a few side dishes."

Wes exchanged glances with Jennifer, and she knew exactly what he was thinking. He'd predicted it wouldn't be long before Emma invited the sisters to the house for supper, so Willy's mayoral campaign wouldn't be far behind. Just the thought of Frances and Fanny being a part of all the hoopla brought a smile to her face.

"That's the smile I've been waiting to see," Wes said, giving her a hug. "It's the one straight from your heart."

At that moment, it seemed to Jennifer the whole world was smiling, and it felt wonderful.